The Limpid Series

Black or with Sugar?
Windchimes and Sirens
Light and Sweet

Murder Bird

Jazmin Galloway

First Edition

1 3 5 7 9 10 8 6 4 2

Cover designed by Jazmin Galloway

ISBN: 978-1-7351652-2-6

To my kin.

"Those who dream by day are cognizant of many things which escape those who dream only by night."

~ Edgar Allen Poe

CHAPTER 1

The boat surges forward through the shifting sea. Jaamini sits with her legs pulled up on the bed, her mind reeling with possibilities. If she makes it to shore, which of course she will, what will she say?

Hey, Father! Remember that thing you told me I couldn't do all my life? Well I came to do just that.

No, that isn't any good. He'll most likely shoot her the instant he sees her, daughter or not.

"Mistress Jaamini?" a man calls from the doorway. She untangles her limbs and flips herself toward his direction.

"What is it?"

"We are approaching land now. You should start repacking."

"Gracias. You may go." He nods, the door clicking softly behind him. Her stomach flips as she looks out the large window. A school of pink salmon swims by.

Standing on shaky legs, she steadies her breathing.

"Nothing's gonna stop me. No, sir," she says, swaying with the boat as they wash over a particularly big wave. She runs to the window, looking up at the dark sky.

"Aw, just my luck! It's going to rain." She pulls away from the window and starts throwing her clothes messily into her giant white suitcase. Her family emblem—a gold crown with a big *R* in the middle—shines up at her. Her fingers ghost over it, hazel eyes misting with happy tears.

"You've treated me well. I'm going to prove to you that anyone can do good work. Anyone. Even *me*." She leans down and kisses the crown before snapping her suitcase closed. Her heels click on the floor, the hallway light bright on her cream skin. Wavy hair floats down her back, her taupe dress trailing around her ankles.

People bow their heads as she walks by. They stop and move out of her way. Her suitcase rolls loudly behind her. She stops at the doors to the deck and looks to the closest person. The woman jolts when their eyes connect.

"Bring me an umbrella?" she asks, and the woman hurriedly runs back into the jacket closet to grab one. She comes back out with a pearly white umbrella that matches Jaamini's suitcase.

"Thank you," Jaamini says, beaming. Then she clambers up the stairs to the deck. She opens the umbrella and blocks the sun from her glossy skin. She doesn't want to swelter in her heavy dress. The porter from earlier stops talking and nods his head at her. Jaamini nods back, fluttering her dark lashes.

She stands by the railing looking out to the seagulls as they cross the sky. One of her hands wraps tightly around the railing.

She closes her eyes, breathing in the salty smell of the sea and the bit of smoke rising through the air from the crew's cigars.

"Right there is it all. Los Angeles," a man says. His heavy Spanish accent doesn't sound suited for the English that tumbles from his lips.

"*Sí*. I have waited many years to venture to America," Jaamini says. He nods and moves along the deck, rolling two crates. Jaamini smiles as the sky rumbles.

The boat docks, rocking as it lowers the stairs to let the crowd of Spaniards to the deck.

"Make sure you grab all your belongings and family members!" one of the crewmen calls. Jaamini rolls her eyes and follows after the throng of people spilling off the stairs.

Her heels catch on the wooden planks. With a grumble, she steps out of them. Her dainty white stockings soak up the dirt as she steps along the pier.

Her shoulders drop when a black car rolls to a stop in front of her, and the door pops open.

"Really? Ma sent you?" Jaamini asks. The man steps out of the car with his arms folded.

"I very well can't have you head there alone."

She shakes her head and steps into the black Jeep. A man made purely of muscle grabs her suitcase and puts it in the trunk. Jaamini puts on her heels as her guardian steps into the vehicle after her.

"You thought your *mother* of all people would send you to America *alone* after what happened to The Grandfather?"

Jaamini glares at the man in front of her. He's grown into his square jaw and black eyes. His hair is buzzed short, and he doesn't wear a grill anymore.

"Don't call him *The Grandfather*; it makes him sound scary or something. He's my pa-pop, and he wasn't evil."

Nico raises a brow at her and sinks back into the gray leather seat. "Your pa-pop, as you put it, was an evil man, and he was the grandfather of every Reyes."

Jaamini scoffs, looking out the window. "He didn't deserve to die like that," she mumbles. Nico is quiet for a second.

"We all deserve to die. Sorry to put it so harshly, *princesa*," Nico says after a breath.

"I'm not a princess. More importantly, I'm not *your* princess, so don't call me that. Secondly, what happened to you, Nico? What about our cause? Our family?" Jaamini asks.

Nico chuckles dryly. He pulls a metal comb from his inner suit pocket and runs it through his goatee.

"Life happened, *mi amor*. Things I would never repeat even if I tried."

Jaamini picks at her nails. Her gut twists. "I wouldn't want you to," she whispers, pulling her eyes from her glittery white nails.

"And what's with you? Why are you here?" Nico asks.

She steals a glance at the man by her side and sighs. "It's time, Nico. It's time I do what every other blood in my family did."

His eyes go dark, and his hands ball into fists. "Are you cured?" he asks.

"What—"

"Are you cured?" he growls.

Jaamini crosses her arms over her chest. "No, I am not cured. But also, why would that matter?"

He waves a hand, and the driver pulls the car over. Taking off his seat belt, he faces Jaamini fully.

"I refuse to let you—"

"Forget your refusal. I am a grown woman and can make choices without the consent of others," Jaamini says.

"A grown woman at the age of sixteen?" he asks with a smirk. She unravels her arms and slips over to his side of the Jeep. She smiles languidly at him, and his smirk drops.

"Yeah. Wanna see?" she asks coyly. He coughs. A blush

covers his cheeks.

"You're kidding, right?" he asks. Jaamini pulls back, laughing. Nico shakes his head.

"You should see your face! You look so surprised. Nico, I am a woman regardless of my age. I have proved myself as such."

"Yes, yes, I heard all about it. The Reyes protégé who took out more than a yard's worth of soldiers," Nico recites knowingly.

"Good, my reputation proceeds me." Jaamini smiles smugly. Nico waves to the driver, and he pulls them back into traffic.

"Look, I will let your father be the judge of what you do. But I am telling you, being on the training grounds in Spain and being here in America on the streets are vastly different things. No amount of training is going to prepare you for what horrors you'll see here. Nada," he says.

Jaamini gulps. Her eyes drift to the swaying palm trees and the playing children. A man is even outside grilling. Nothing looks out of the ordinary. Nothing but the houses. Everywhere she looks are one-story homes with a porch and white shingle walls.

It looks quiet until they get farther into the city where the shopping district rolls in.

She sees small boutiques in the middle of all the shopping and partying chaos.

Then she feels it: the change in pace, the shift in people. They are wary to walk the street where the penthouse is.

The car slows to a stop in front of the apartment building, the sides of it lit up like a casino.

Jaamini gapes at it in awe.

"We're here. Your future, whether it's good or bad."

She slaps his arm and rolls her eyes. Nico always

manages to take the mystique away before she can enjoy it. Jaamini jumps out the car before he can even unbuckle his seat belt.

CHAPTER 2

Jaamini walks toward the two men standing in front of the building.

In front of her is a walkway suited for the rich, with smooth gravel all the way up to glass double doors. She has to remind herself that the shiny gold building is more than just a home. She never saw anything like this in Spain.

Jaamini waits for Nico. He thrusts the handle of her suitcase at her.

She takes the handle and storms up to the door, her hands shaking.

"You ready?" Nico asks softly. His tall frame is doubled over just so he can reach her.

"Of course I'm ready. Open the door."

He sighs and reaches for the handle, pulling it open and waiting for her.

Jaamini steps into the air-conditioned building. Hazel eyes scan the walls. A clean, smooth, black marble counter is in the front with a man twisting a key ring over a finger.

He jumps up when he spots them. He stares at Nico with confusion. His eyes trail over Jaamini's dress, her heels, her pretty blond hair.

"You brought home a who—"

"No!" Nico barks, cutting the man off.

Jaamini frowns and walks up to the counter. *Control yourself.* A smile stretches softly across her face. "I am not a worker. My name is Jaamini. Who are you?"

He raises a brow, looking her up and down for another long second. His hands flick and fumble with the key ring.

"He's not important. Come on," Nico says.

Jaamini waits another moment with the man staring at her funny. With a shrug, she follows Nico down the hall toward the elevator. A few men sit around a love seat counting money. One of them winks at her as she passes.

The elevator is cramped compared to the hallway. It squeezes the two next to each other.

"Smells like cheese," Jaamini mumbles to fill the silence. A second passes, and Nico raises his arm. Jaamini glances at him through her curled lashes.

He takes a deep sniff of his sleeve before putting his arm back down. She holds back her chuckle and stares straight ahead at the gold doors.

"Now—" Nico starts but stops when the doors open. Jaamini waits for him to talk, but he doesn't. He darts into the hall and straight to the closest door.

Jaamini trudges behind him. Her suitcase rolls along the tiled floor smoothly. Nico raps on the door roughly and waits.

A voice sounds on the other side, muffled even to Jaamini's ears.

"It's Nico," Nico calls. "Sir," he adds as an afterthought. For a second, Jaamini's imagination runs wild.

What if Father answers the door? What will I say to him? She isn't supposed to be here for him anyway. *What if he decides to just shoot me and get it over with?*

The door opens to reveal a man with striking good looks. Well, she thinks he's a man.

His slender eyes are bright blue and slanted. His white-blond hair tumbles down his back and ends in a fading green.

The man folds his arms over his chest.

"What exactly are you doing with this young woman?" he asks. His voice, though booming, is calming.

"She came here to see Pinky." Nico turns to Jaamini, who smiles sweetly.

"Hi," she says.

The man smiles back. "Hello. What do you want with him?"

Jaamini shrugs. It's strange explaining to strangers why she dropped everything and left home. The man nods slowly and steps out of the doorframe.

Nico steps forward and is halted by the older man.

"You're not coming in. Boss's orders. He doesn't want to talk to you right now."

"How could you know that?" Nico says, his voice gruff, inflated.

"It's fine, Nico. You didn't even have to bring me here," Jaamini says. Nico rolls his eyes and folds his arms over his chest.

"Be careful," he mouths and grabs her suitcase. Jaamini nods and steps into the apartment.

"Right this way." The man stalks off into the house with ease. His back is straight and relaxed, like she isn't dangerous. Maybe to a man in his line of work she isn't.

The two of them stop in front of the last door in the hallway. A wall length window captures the view of the bright sky, and an abundance of sunlight pours onto the floor.

Jaamini looks down at the people walking the streets, bouncing from place to place. There are many interesting-looking restaurants down this strip of street.

"What's your name?" the man asks, turning to her.

"Jaamini."

He opens the door and steps two feet in. "You have a visitor. A young woman named Jaamini."

Jaamini steps in after him. The walls are lined with bookshelves; what's on them makes her shudder.

"Tony, who in the world do you know—"

Tony steps out of the way, exposing Jaamini to him. The man frowns and stands, placing his hands in his pockets.

"Why are you here?" he asks. Jaamini's eyes never leave the wall of plastic-wrapped severed fingers—more specifically, pinkies.

"Why do you have these?" she asks.

Pinky looks at his wall and then back at her. Two fingers push black shades up the bridge of his nose.

"How long did you travel?"

Jaamini steps toward the rack and starts counting them. "About five hours or so. Not very long, actually," she mumbles. Pinky sighs deeply and comes to stand by her side.

"Your mother?" he asks.

"She says hi."

The room is silent.

Jaamini's heart hammers in her chest. She turns to Pinky. Although he isn't looking at her, she can feel the intensity of his presence.

Being around him is enough to make people want to bolt.

"Why are you here?" he asks again. This time he turns fully toward her and removes his shades.

A startled gasp ripples through the room.

The two glance at Tony, wearing matching expressions, then they disregard him.

"Your hair's still pink," Jaamini says with a nod. Pinky pinches the bridge of his nose and runs a hand over his buzz cut. His fingers bear a link of brass knuckles.

"Why are you here?" he says again. His eyes blaze with repressed anger. Jaamini steps closer.

"You have a new tattoo? Is it a bird or something?" She reaches up to touch it, and his hand snatches hers out of the air. Tony moves, smacking into a chair.

The loud noise startles the two, and they break apart.

"Mini, answer the question," Pinky deadpans. Jaamini's shoulders sag, and she gives in.

"I'm not here for you; I'm here for the gang."

Pinky stands frozen. His eyes are glazed over and calculating. She waits with bated breath. Her feet ache to bolt. She fists the sides of her dress.

"No," he says and turns away.

Balking, Jaamini stops him from returning to his desk.

"*No?* Are you out of it?"

"*Mi corazón*, you will not." He sits in his seat and starts shuffling through papers. His lack of regard toward her feelings makes her all the more determined. Her brows draw inward.

"*Mi corazón?*" Tony repeats like the words are foreign on his lips. Jaamini and Pinky look at him again, and she realizes why the man is so confused.

"He's my father," Jaamini clarifies. Tony blinks rapidly, then points between the two of them. His mouth drops open, and his eyes go wide with disbelief.

"You . . . no way. I have to tell Adelio." He shakes his head and moves toward the door.

"No. This doesn't leave this room," Pinky says.

Tony raises a brow. "C'mon. There's no way I'm keeping

this to myself."

"You will, or you won't live to tell the secret anyway."

Jaamini glares at her father. "What do you mean by secret? Why didn't he know about me?" Jaamini asks. Pinky looks pointedly at his daughter. He shuffles through a few more papers before sliding a manilla folder to her side of his desk.

Jaamini looks at the chock-full package and almost growls.

"You've got to be pulling my leg. I am not leaving! You owe me!"

Pinky's hand slams down on the desk. "You're going home!" he shouts.

"No! What's your deal? Everyone in the family has come to serve the South Sanz."

He tsks, throwing his head back. His shoes tap against the floor as he paces back and forth.

"It's because of your heart," he says.

Jaamini stops glaring, her face dropping to what could only be clarified as disappointment.

Oh, she thinks, running a hand through her hair.

"I'm sorry, but I can't allow you to join. Not like that," Pinky says.

Jaamini steps away from the desk, her hands fiddling with her dress. "I'll leave."

Pinky hesitates before raising the package toward her.

"It's fine. Mom gave me money," she says, her eyes downcast. Pinky shrugs, dropping the folder but keeping his hand raised. Jaamini looks into his eyes.

"It was nice seeing you, Dad."

"Mini . . ." Pinky says. He frowns when she ignores him and steps out the door. He doesn't call for her again when she enters the hallway. The front door shuts with a distinct click.

Nico pushes off the wall with his hands in his pockets.

CHAPTER 3

"Where are we headed then, hmm?" Nico asks. Jaamini grins, the light in her eyes dancing.

"Let's head to my aunt's."

Nico nods and grabs the handle to her suitcase. He swipes his card for the elevator, and they wait.

"You seem ticked off. Does this have anything to do with your dad?" he asks.

"Who else?"

He shrugs, then steals a glance in her direction. "It could have something to do with a *novio* back at home," he says and steps so hard into the elevator his shoes thud against it. Jaamini keeps her opinion to herself about his obvious discomfort.

"I don't have a boyfriend," she says. Jaamini smiles when she sees his shoulders relax.

"Good . . . no, I don't mean good. I mean, the car . . . no, not the car. I—"

"It's okay, Nico. I know what you meant," she says before covering her smirk with her hair. Jealousy is kind of cute on him.

"So where are you staying if not with your dad?" he asks. The elevator doors open before they hit the bottom. A group of three close into the tiny space.

The one leading the group is a redhead Jaamini remembers vividly.

"Uncle Rio?" she calls.

"Mini?" He chuckles and turns toward her. His machete hangs on his waist. He rolls his shoulders, stretching the fabric of his long sleeve. Jaamini nods at him, and he nods back. A big lopsided grin grows on his cheeks.

"You've got to be, I dunno, seventeen by now."

"Close enough," she says. The elevator doors slide open, and they step out. She faces him, knowing there's a lot he has to say to her, or maybe even ask, though she doesn't want to answer.

"How's it?" He nods his chin toward her. She sighs and runs her hands into her hair to massage her scalp.

"It's fine. Why's everyone so worried? I'm not dead."

Rio cracks his neck and pulls a dagger from his sleeve. "Your our precious little medallion. We don't want anything to happen to you. If you were to go, who knows what Pinky would do." He reaches out a hand. Jaamini shakes it and nods once more. Rio takes off with his crew in tow, leaving nothing behind. His blades gleam in the light.

"You're cool with him?" Nico asks, coming to her side.

"Not really. He and my father go way back. Way before my birth."

Nico takes her hand and drags her out of the building. She notes the men traveling up the emergency stairway before they duck back into the comfort of the car.

"I'll call your aunt."

Jaamini looks out the window and watches the houses. On their way, they pass a church that looks too familiar to home.

"You been to a new church yet?" Jaamini asks, craning her neck to see the cross standing proud on top of its roof.

"No. I wouldn't go to any holy place but the one at home."

"Shame." Jaamini notes the way people stand in front of buildings snapping pictures. Others jog, and a few girls play with a jump rope in a park.

Jaamini peers ahead of them to the row houses they pull up alongside.

"She lives here?" she asks.

"Yes." Nico jumps out of the car like a child and holds a hand out to her. Jaamini disregards his hand and jumps out for herself.

"Thanks," she says, stalking up to the child on the steps. She takes in her red-brown hair and her brown eyes. The girl looks up from her phone and nods a greeting. "You must be Honey," Jaamini says.

"How do you know me?" Honey asks. Jaamini smiles unconsciously and snickers. Honey stands up, pushing her phone into her pocket. The two size each other up for a long moment.

"I'm your cousin," Jaamini answers. Honey looks at her with lowered lids.

"Yeah, and I like frogs," Honey says. For a second the girls stand there, unblinking. Then they burst into laughter.

"It sounded better in my head," Honey says. Jaamini nods.

"Would have sounded better if you explained yourself a little bit as well."

Honey shrugs. The front door to the house opens up.

Jaamini looks up the steps of the little house and into the eyes of her aunt. The woman smiles and waves.

"I hope you didn't have a bad trip," she says. Jaamini wraps her arms around the woman's torso and gives her a big squeeze.

"No. My trip here wasn't all unpleasant. The crew was very nice to me. "

"Good," Helena says. Jaamini follows her aunt through the house to the living room. A man sits on the couch with his eyes trained on his phone. His long limbs stretch from the couch across the top of the coffee table. His dark brown hair is pulled back into two cornrows that hang down over his shoulders. His tanned skin is clear. He glances in her direction and looks back at his phone.

"Cousin Adelio?" she asks, coming a bit closer. He turns his attention to her for a second, and his mouth drops open. He throws his phone on the couch and jumps up. "Hi!" she shrieks, wrapping her arms around his lean torso. He hugs her back tightly.

"It's been a long time, Little Cuz," he says. The vibration of his deep voice rattles her teeth. She removes her head from his chest and grins at him. He grins back and pats her head. "How was the trip here? Why are you here?"

"I came to see you guys," she says, pulling back to sit on the couch. Adelio follows her and plops back in his spot.

"Somehow I don't believe that." He looks up at Nico. It's been so long since she's seen him that she can't stop staring. "What?" he asks finally.

"How old are you now? Eighteen or something?" Jaamini asks. Adelio shakes his head.

"I'm twenty . . . and I'm married now."

Her eyes go wide, and she turns to him excitedly. *What beautiful woman snatched him up?* Aunt Helena hands her a bottled water.

"Thanks, Auntie," she says without looking toward her.

Her eyes are glued to Adelio's face expectantly. He flashes the screen of his phone toward her.

It takes a few seconds for her to look down. The unopened bottle drops from her hand, and her eyes go impossibly wider.

"I just met him," she says.

Adelio looks down at the picture of himself and Tony.

"You were at the penthouse?" he asks, his eyes telling stories she can't understand.

"Yes?" she says, unsure of his reaction.

"Why?"

"My father—"

His brows furrow, and it's his turn to look at her in confusion. "Your father was at the penthouse . . . with Tony?" he asks. She nods. His eyes lower into a squint. "Your father is . . . ?"

Jaamini blinks slowly before a frown etches into her face. "You don't know either," she says, disappointed. Helena takes this as a chance to enter the conversation.

"A lot of stuff was happening when you were born, sweetie. No one told him who your father is."

Adelio looks between them. His eyes go dark, and he stands up. He leans back on the balls of his feet, shoulders tensing up.

"Pinky?" he asks. Jaamini nods. He sighs, looking down at his shoes. She looks at the Puma RS Dreamers and nods in appreciation.

"How . . . ? Why . . . ?" Adelio sighs, shaking his head. "He likes women?" he asks finally.

Jaamini's face sours, and she starts laughing. She runs a hand through her hair, then opens her water and takes a few large gulps. Her eyes glance to Nico, who leans against the living room wall.

"He's straight, unlike someone," she jokes, her eyes turning back to Adelio.

A grin stretches across Adelio's face, and he sits down again. "Yeah, I wasn't too sure. Never seen him with anyone."

Jaamini relaxes into the couch and nods Nico over. He shakes his head and continues to rest against the wall.

"So how is Marie?" Helena asks.

"She's doing well. Misses Dad, though," Jaamini says. Adelio shudders.

"Yeah, I'm sure," he mumbles to himself.

Jaamini rolls her eyes at him and turns back to Helena. "Can you set up a meeting with the boss for me?" The room goes still. The only sound is the soft breaths of the fan sitting in the corner of the room. Helena's brows knit together, and her mouth opens and closes.

"Of course I can. But you can just see him for dinner."

"It's work related," Jaamini clarifies. Helena blanches and scratches her head.

"I will let him know then." She stands and takes out her phone. Her footsteps retreat into the room not too far off.

"You're such a liar, Little Cuz." Adelio sighs. He stands up and waves for Nico to take a seat. Nico looks at the couch and groans before going to sit by Jaamini.

Adelio brings a chair from deeper in the house to the living room and sits down.

"Why are you trying to join the gang?" he asks once he is seated and comfortable. Jaamini shrugs. He pinches his mouth into a thin line. She holds her ground against him. "Fine. I will ask him myself," Adelio says, resting his back against the chair. He smirks at her obvious discomfort. Jaamini pulls at the fabric of her dress.

CHAPTER 4

Jaamini looks up at Adelio with a deep sigh.

"Why train for a job you can't have?" He raises a brow, leaning forward with his elbows propped up on his legs.

"What do you mean?" Jaamini stops picking at the threads on the end of her dress. "I trained at the academy for this position. A seat at the table, if you will."

Adelio frowns. "They trained you?" he asks. Jaamini nods.

"Everyone in the Reyes family was trained at the age of three to be a Right Hand to your family. I am surprised you didn't know."

He stares at the door where his mother disappeared. "I was gone for a very long time from all of this. I just got back into it about two years ago."

"Really? They just let you go?" Jaamini asks. Adelio chuckles. Helena enters the room with a sly smile covering her beautiful slender face.

"Your appointment is for early tomorrow. That's when the most important business goes down. I would be careful if I were you."

Jaamini sits up straighter. "Thank you, Auntie."

Helena pulls Jaamini into an embrace. "No, thank *you*. He's staying the night tonight." She starts snickering at Adelio's face.

He groans. "Mom, why?"

She rolls her eyes and looks at Nico. "So who are you again?" she asks. Her hands sit patiently on her hips.

"Oh, sorry. My name's Nico. Miss Marie asked me to watch Jaamini while she's here. Or at least get her to someone who could watch her."

Helena sticks her hand out to him. He shakes it and smiles awkwardly.

Helena grabs another chair and brings it into the living room.

"So, Mini, you want to be a gangster." She cracks a smile at her niece. Jaamini smiles back.

"It's only right. What else would I do with my skill set?"

"What is your skill set?" Adelio asks.

"Shooting, stabbing, punching . . . bombs?" She shrugs at his gaping mouth and wide eyes. "There's other stuff, but it's a bit more complicated than that," she says. Adelio scoffs and glances down at his phone screen. "Anyway, how have you been, Auntie?"

"Fine. But really, Jaamini, it's not as fun as you may think. Being in a gang, I mean." Footsteps thump against the floor as Honey runs into the living room and plops into her mother's lap.

The air in the room is thick, swirling with tense energy. She looks around between the adults.

"What's everyone talking about?" she asks. Her curious brown eyes are wide and expectant. Helena rolls her eyes and hugs her daughter.

"Nothing that concerns you. Would you like to start on

dinner?"

"Mom, it's like three o'clock."

"A great time to knock out those dishes."

Honey glares at her mother and stands up. She looks at Adelio for aid, and he shrugs. Grumbling, the teen stomps out of the living room and disappears down the hall.

"You ain't have to do her like that, Mom," Adelio says. Helena shrugs, her eyes on Jaamini.

"I am not joining the gang for fun. I am doing it out of duty," Jaamini clarifies. Adelio snickers next to her. She pins him with a cold stare. He looks back at his phone.

"You can use this time to break from tradition. You don't have to be part of the gang," Helena says.

"I do. It is my responsibility and my goal." She doesn't get to finish, as a tall young boy enters the living room.

"Excuse me. Mom?"

Helena looks at the boy and smiles at him, her eyes dazzling with a motherly gleam. "Yes, Tito?"

"May I open the donuts?"

"Absolutely. But you have to help Honey wash those dishes."

He stares at her for a long time, unblinking, then frowns and nods. "Yes, ma'am." The boy scurries off without looking at anyone else in the room.

"Who's that?" Jaamini asks, an answer buzzing around her head.

"That's obviously her other son," Adelio says mockingly. Jaamini nods.

"Is he Honey's twin or something?" Jaamini asks. Helena hums.

"What were you saying about goal—" The bell for the house rings, cutting her off. Sighing, Helena throws her arms up. "Hold that thought," she says, stalking out of the room.

"A word of advice, Little Cuz," Adelio says. Jaamini looks at him. She is getting tired; her trip here filled her with so much anxiety she didn't sleep a wink. She stares at Adelio blankly. "Don't try to live up to shadows that are bigger than your own."

Jaamini weighs his advice in her head. *Shadows bigger than my own,* she thinks with unfocused eyes glued to the wall.

Helena enters the living room with her mouth set in a thin line. She folds her arms over her chest.

"I thought you were going home," a man grumbles. Adelio tenses at the voice and spins in his seat to look at Pinky. Jaamini barely registers his voice.

"Look at me, child."

Automatically, she looks up at her father, startled by his presence.

"I never said I was going home. I just left you." She stands and approaches him. Her heart thumps wildly in her chest. *He is so unreasonable.*

Pinky groans and pulls the shades from his face. Adelio gasps.

Tony moves around them and takes a seat on the couch.

"I know, right?" Jaamini hears him mumble into the otherwise silent room.

Pinky and Jaamini stare at each other, their conversation happening through their eyes.

"I am joining regardless of how you feel," she says aloud.

"Going behind my back like this is unacceptable," Pinky answers.

"Whatever do you mean?" she asks, mimicking his stance. Pinky grits his teeth, mumbling under his breath. "Excuse me! I am your kid," she says, her voice rising.

"Who do you think you're telling? You're just as insufferable and stubborn as your mother." He shakes his head and looks around the room. His eyes land on Nico, and he raises a brow. "What the hell are you doing here?" he asks, passing Jaamini. Her hand shoots out and grabs his arm.

"He is my guide as per my mother's request. You got a problem?" she asks, inclining her head up at him. Pinky's look toward her is murderous.

"No," he says after many long moments of silence. He rips his forearm from her hand and leans down toward her. His breath fans over her face. "Be careful, Mini. The big Sanz is not in a very good mood right now."

"Thank you for the heads-up," she says. Pinky pulls back, shaking his head.

"Are you eating dinner here?" he asks. Curious about his sudden drop in anger, Jaamini looks to her aunt for confirmation.

"Yes," Jaamini says after Helena's nod of approval.

"Give me your phone."

Jaamini fishes for it, passing it over without hesitation. Her father puts in his number and drops it in her hand. She stares at his new tattoos.

"It's an acronym. For my favorite poet."

"Edgar Allen Poe?" she asks, pulling his hand into her hand. "Raven . . ." she mumbles, reading the letters spanning across his knuckles.

"Yes," he says. Helena comes over to peer at his hand, her eyes more focused on his brass knuckles than the tattoo.

"How's this been working for you?" she asks excitedly.

"You're a psycho," he says.

"That was established decades ago." Helena waves his comment off nonchalantly.

"They work better than your knife collection."

Her head snaps up, eyes locking with his. "Wanna bet?" she asks. He smirks.

"I'd kill you in seconds," Pinky says.

"Doubt it. Last time I checked you can't even find a replacement for me." A smirk folds over her features. Pinky sucks his teeth—a very unnatural reaction, in Jaamini's opinion.

She looks between the two of them.

"Don't even ask, kid," Pinky says before Jaamini can ask what she's talking about.

Dropping his hand in defiance, Jaamini steals her aunt's chair and pouts to herself. Curiosity eats away at her, and in seconds she's a sighing mess.

Helena backs out of Pinky's space.

"I admit it's been slow, but there are so many other things going on. He should give up," Pinky says.

"Mom!" Honey yells from the kitchen. Everybody jumps, looking toward the hallway.

Pinky chuckles dryly and enters the hall.

"I will show myself out. Tony, you're relieved for the night," he says. Tony nods once and sighs when the front door closes.

"I thought he would never let me go home. Always working," Tony mumbles. Adelio kisses his cheek.

"As long as you're not on the field, it shouldn't be much of a problem."

"How'd I become his lackey anyway? It's like that time of my life is all a blur."

Adelio rests his cheek on top of Tony's head. His brown eyes glance to Jaamini, who stares down at her hands.

"You all right, Cuz?" he asks. Jaamini is dead silent, lost in thought.

"How could she be all right? Her dad is a meanie," Tony says.

Nico snorts. "She can be pretty mean herself," he says.

Her eyes refocus after that, and she flips him off. "I try to be nice to everyone. But *someone* is always pushing my buttons," she says. Nico raises his hands in surrender, grinning like a hyena.

"Mom is starting dinner. She wants everyone to know that," Tito says from the living room archway. He keeps his gaze low and rocks on the sides of his feet.

"Thanks, Tito," Adelio says.

"I'm Jaamini, your cousin. Marie's daughter," Jaamini adds, hoping to get his attention. The boy looks away from the ground to give her a once-over, then sinks his gaze back to the ground.

"Tito," he whispers. Jaamini takes that as enough conversation.

"It's nice to finally meet you."

He nods again, scratching lightly at his forearm.

"He's just shy around new people. He'll warm up to you soon," Adelio says as if he isn't standing five feet away.

"I can see that. Thanks," she says sharply. Adelio and Tony start chuckling. Nico hides his grin behind a yawn.

She rolls her eyes and looks back at the archway to see her cousin has disappeared. He must be quiet on his feet for her not to have noticed.

Helena returns to the room and scoops up her phone.

"Would you like for me to get you a hotel room?" Helena asks.

"She can stay with us if she wants," Tony says before Jaamini can answer.

"You two are too loud at night," Helena says quickly. Jaamini looks between the two of them, amused.

"I don't care much where I sleep as long as it's not far."

"Then stay with us. We can head to our place after dinner," Tony says.

"Cool," Jaamini says.

CHAPTER 5

Jaamini yawns into the fold of her arm as they leave the living room for the dinner table. Helena pulls out her chair, and she quietly thanks her. Her limbs are growing weak with exhaustion, and she just hopes to be attentive during dinner.

Tito enters the living room with his head down, scooting a separate chair next to his own. He looks around the table, most likely counting to make sure there are enough. Jaamini herself counted the chairs and looks to the extra chair in confusion.

"You're in luck, Little Cuz. You're on my side of the table," Adelio jokes, leaning his face into his palm.

"Who's going to be on the other side?" Jaamini asks. Adelio opens his mouth, but it closes instantly. He glares above her head with flared nostrils.

The room fills with the scent of lemon and smoke. She turns to look at the man behind her. He smirks when their eyes meet.

"Hello, Uncle Sullivan," she says, walking up to him. They hug briefly.

"Welcome to our little home," Sullivan says.

"Thank you. It's pretty quaint."

He chuckles and pulls his twins into a tight hug. They all sit at the table while Helena and Honey set the table up.

It's been a long time since Jaamini sat down at a dinner table to eat. She doesn't normally do so at home in Spain.

"So, Mini, how are your mother and grandfather?"

Jaamini frowns. Her eyes shift to Nico, and he shrugs.

"Mother is doing well. Grandfather passed a few months ago."

Her uncle sits back against his chair, his hands clasped together. "My condolences. Have you had the funeral?"

Jaamini nods.

He hums with an intense gaze. "He was a great man."

She nods, looking down at her empty plate. Her grandfather was a menace to society. A great man, her foot. She still loved him regardless, but he needed to get his priorities in check.

"Is the academy still running smoothly?" Sullivan asks.

"Yes. Mother is in charge now, and things are . . . different."

Sullivan nods. "I would assume so. She was never one for violence."

Jaamini scoffs. Her mother is a fool. What they're supposed to be doing isn't violence; it's art, a form of teaching, tradition, and protection for the young.

"You seem to have different views."

"My mother and I have never seen eye to eye about traditions," Jaamini says.

Sullivan takes the fork from beside his plate and plucks the top of it. The resounding vibrations flow through the room, drawing everyone's eyes to him.

"Murder is a hard pill to swallow." His arm is

immediately swatted by Helena as she and Honey take a seat at the table. He raises a brow but otherwise does not engage his wife.

Jaamini looks between the two of them with a sad smile. It would have been nice if her parents had the same kind of relationship her aunt and uncle have. Maybe then she wouldn't be such a brat. She shakes her head at the thought.

"Lead us in prayer, Sullivan," Helena says. He takes his son's and his wife's hands. They all bow their heads, and he leads the prayer. Jaamini utters her own words of prayer silently.

They break into a quiet dinner. Everyone is absorbed in their plates. She's surprised to hear the amount of notifications going off on everyone's phones and not see a single person reach for them.

She follows suit and does not reach for her phone though it buzzes on and off. By the time she's eaten half of her plate, her eyes close every few seconds.

"Jaamini," Adelio says softly, shaking her awake. She jolts, gripping his hand and twisting his arm. He grunts in pain and taps at the table. Jaamini lets go, sheepishly muttering apologies.

"I hadn't noticed I was dozing," she mumbles. Adelio rubs at his elbow and shoulder.

"It's whatever. We're going to head out now so you can get some sleep." She eyes his unfinished plate, and her face warms in embarrassment.

"I can wait—"

"No thanks. You deserve to sleep on a bed, not a chair."

She nods. "Thank you for the food, Auntie." Helena smiles at her through sips from her glass. "It was nice meeting you two," Jaamini says, looking toward her younger cousins. Honey smiles, and Tito nods curtly. His plate is a lot more interesting than her face.

Jaamini almost laughs at the irony.

"Talk to you tomorrow, Uncle Sullivan."

"Have Tony drive you. He knows where to find me."

"Will do," Jaamini says, covering her mouth as she yawns. Adelio helps her out of her seat. Her leftovers are stuffed into Tupperware and pushed under Tony's arm. He chuckles when she looks at it, barely able to raise her arms, let alone walk straight.

Nico follows suit in saying goodbye to everyone at the table, then follows them outside.

"I have her suitcase in the back," he says. Jaamini stares sleepily through the window at the driver. He glances at Nico and reaches down. The trunk pops on the car, but he doesn't get out.

"Who is that?" Jaamini mutters.

She lets Tony walk her toward a large sparkling Jeep. It isn't literally sparkling, but under the streetlight she can see a glistening layer of sparkles covering its black exterior.

"It's pretty," she says, eyes closing slowly. Adelio helps her into the back seat and pops on her seat belt.

"Yeah, sure it is. But it's the second one, and Tony should have just gotten something different," Adelio says.

"They don't make cars like this no more," Tony whines, jumping into the driver's seat. The car rumbles to life. Nico drops the suitcase into the trunk and says his goodbyes.

"Later," Jaamini calls—or at least she thinks she does—before the smooth driving lulls her into the vacuum of sleep.

*****

Jaamini opens her eyes to a large white building. The sun is warm on her face, wind jostling her dress around her knees. She sighs into the morning air.

"You coming?" a woman asks in a singsong voice. Jaamini looks at the older woman. Her hazel eyes are bright and round. She waves her over, and Jaamini follows down a dirt path that stops just before a large field of sunflowers.

"When will I see Dad?" Jaamini asks. Her voice is light and airy. The older woman looks at her with a big smile full of straight white teeth. Her long black dress hugs a tall, slender frame.

"You can see him whenever you want, darling! You're a woman now. Sixteen is the perfect time to travel and see the world."

Jaamini follows her through the long swaying flowers.

The smell of grass pungent in her nose, her fingertips gloss over each stem she steps past. Her breathing is deep and relaxed.

"Mother?" she calls to the woman. Her mother doesn't respond, just keeps walking faster while her distance stays the same. Her blond hair flows behind her like an ocean.

The sun blinds Jaamini as she tries to keep pace, but she loses her in the patch of flowers. Jaamini stops walking, looking at the endless hills of tilting and swaying flowers.

She turns to the closest one and pulls it to her. Inhaling deeply, she closes her eyes and lets her tears flow freely—tears for her grandfather, her mentor, her friend.

*****

Jaamini yawns awake, stretching her limbs out over soft fabric. She smacks her lips and rolls onto her stomach, then sluggishly raises her head and opens her eyes.

The room is chilly and gray. The walls around her are painted ash, and the bed is fitted with a gray sheet. Her pillow rises, the shape of her head slowly vanishing. She chuckles and drags herself upward.

Trying to remember her dream, she wipes at the wetness on her face, but nothing comes back, just a dark splotch of time.

Checking the time on her phone, she frowns. *Five o'clock.* She's still waking up like she has to go to the academy.

How upsetting.

She stands and pops open her suitcase. Shuffling through the top few dresses, she pulls out a long red body-con. The weather here isn't as pleasant as her rainbow-colored wardrobe, but she'll make do.

She throws everything she needs on top of the white suitcase and closes the latches. She stares down at the medallion logo on the top and kisses two fingers to it. They slip down the length of it before she pulls away.

With more excitement than necessary, she opens the door to the closet and peers around. There are no clothes, just a little box with writing on top that says, "Big weapons—just kidding." Jaamini stares at it a little longer, her finger twitching to open the sealed cardboard box.

Nope. She would get in so much trouble.

Closing the door, she opens another door which leads to a half bath. She stands in front of the mirror and looks it up and down. It's spotless, just the way she likes.

The sink, though clean, looks unused. She peers at the toilet. It's also spotless and likely hasn't been used much. A fluffy-looking gray cover wraps around the seat. A fresh roll of tissues is stacked in a black basket by its side.

She'd guess Adelio isn't this accommodating, but Tony must be. She leaves the bathroom, flicking off the light switch, and ventures out into the hallway with all her stuff.

She finds the bathroom with the shower easily. She takes a scalding hot shower and washes her hair. It has been far too long since she relaxed like this.

Once she's changed and ready, she folds up her clothes and places them back in her suitcase. Jaamini checks the time on her phone.

Five thirty.

"Now what?" she grumbles to herself, looking around the room.

Nothing to do.

She's bound to get hungry soon.

CHAPTER 6

Jaamini finds her way to the kitchen.

"Good morning," she says, startling Tony. He turns to her, scratching the back of his neck.

"Good morning. You're up early."

"As are you," she quips.

"Hungry?" he asks, sticking a thumb out toward the fridge. She nods. He opens it and pulls out the Tupperware. "You can either eat your leftovers or wait for breakfast. Or you can do both. Whatever you want."

"What are you making for breakfast?" she asks, closing the distance between them.

"Scrambled eggs, bacon, and toast. Sound good?"

"Sounds great." She leans against the counter and watches as he puts coffee grinds into the filter.

"Do you drink coffee?" he asks with a yawn.

"Not normally. I like water more."

He looks at her with raised brows. "You like . . . water? Like, water water?"

Jaamini starts laughing. "Yes, water. You've said it thrice now."

He stands there, unmoving, just staring at her. "What have they done to you?" he mumbles and fills the coffeepot up to the top.

She shakes her head. "What have they done to you? Are you and Adelio about to drink four cups each?"

He looks at her, dumbfounded. "Absolutely," he says.

The two of them bust out laughing while he finishes prepping the pot and turning the machine on. The switch flicks, and it immediately starts to guzzle.

"What kind of cup do you want? Plastic, glass, something fancy, a mug, a thermos?" he asks, quickly turning his back to her and reaching into the cabinet above his head. She spots a bright red cup and grins.

"I want the red M&M's mug."

He briefly looks over his shoulder at her. "Of course you do. Have one back at home?" he asks, pulling down three mugs. The other two are from different brands as well. One is from Star Wars, and the other is from an anime. She draws a blank on the name of it.

"Yes, but mine is green."

He puts her mug in the dispenser on the refrigerator door. The water comes out smoothly, splashing when it hits the bottom of the empty cup.

"How long have you been married to Adelio?" Jaamini asks, setting the two mugs up facing each other.

"About a year now, but I've known him since I was four."

"Really?" she asks, her voice rising an octave.

He hands her the full mug with a smile. "Yes, and he was a terrible child. He had super loose lips and a habit of being impulsive." Tony says.

She sips from her mug, smiling down at it.

"Yeah, I was so young when we met. I can only

remember how he liked to throw sticks at strays and hide under the sink when we played hide-and-seek." Jaamini says. Tony snorts.

"If he could fit under the sink, he would still be doing that." Tony says. Jaamini chuckles at all her memories of playing.

"That must have been before he moved," Tony mumbles to himself.

"He moved?" she asks. Jaamini swallows another gulp; she's thirstier than she thought.

"Yeah. His uncle passed away, and he went to go live with a friend of his."

Jaamini's brows furrow. "Uncle Palo?"

Tony glances at her. "No. Your uncle Sergio."

Jaamini makes a face. Tony seems to realize she never met him.

"You probably weren't old enough to know or meet him by the time he passed," Tony says.

Jaamini nods and finishes off her cup. A sleepy Adelio stumbles into the kitchen and leans on the counter.

"Coffee," he mumbles with a yawn. Tony snickers and passes him the Star Wars mug.

"Make your own." He leaves a groggy Adelio to his own devices and turns the stove on. He places down all his ingredients for breakfast. Jaamini pours herself another mug of water and goes to sit on the couch. Adelio joins her, sipping his hot coffee.

"Adelio?" she says. He holds up a finger and downs the entire cup without stopping. His eyes still aren't open.

How did he even? It must've been boiling hot.

"Yes?"

"Did you know Uncle Sergio well?" she asks. He cracks open an eye and relaxes against the couch.

"Not really. That man slipped in and out of my life until he died. Don't remember a thing."

She looks down at her blurry reflection, her water swishing around in unsteady hands.

"I see," she says finally, but Adelio has already gone back to sleep, his mug clutched tightly in his hands.

Jaamini chuckles and leans back into the gray couch. There's a TV in front of her, but she leaves it off. She wouldn't know what to watch anyway; she didn't grow up with cable.

"Jaamini." She snaps out of her thoughts and looks up at Tony. "Your plate is ready," he says.

"That was fast," she mumbles, standing up.

"Not really. You've been staring at nothing for like fifteen minutes."

She frowns, looking down into her empty cup, then back up to Adelio, who's leaning forward in his own spot on the couch.

She ignores the loss of time. It couldn't have been important if she lost it that easily.

Jaamini takes her plate and another cup of water into the living room and sits down to eat with Tony.

"I'd wake him, but he's normally really grumpy if I wake him up."

Jaamini agrees with a nod. She would be too, especially if she woke up with a crick in her neck and her mouth tasting like black coffee.

Tony sits Adelio up against the couch, as if he heard her thoughts or maybe thought the same thing. It's likely he was imagining waking up with a crick in his neck.

"When will we go see Uncle Sullivan?" Jaamini asks.

"Sulli? Oh, probably after I shower. I still have to pick up your father. He hates driving himself in the morning."

"Does he?" she mumbles, looking away from him. She can't see his expression but assumes he's judging her for her reaction.

"Yeah, he probably needs a few cups of coffee to wake up as well."

She finishes her plate and leans back. "I missed him, but . . . even now all I know about him is what people tell me."

Tony frowns. "It must have been hard growing up a sea away," he says.

"No, my mother is capable. But I've never lived with anyone other than her, so I wouldn't understand growing up with both of my parents."

Tony puts his empty plate down. "Maybe that was fortunate. Your father is good at his job, but the other stuff is debatable."

"I'll take your word for it."

Tony takes their dishes and leaves for his shower, leaving Jaamini alone. Her hands pick at her dress. Her light waves fall over her arms like a blanket.

She's doing this; she's here. With a sigh, she pulls her phone out and calls her mother. The phone rings and rings until the very last ring. Her mother finally answers.

"I thought you died," Marie says.

Jaamini snickers into the phone. "No, I am well. I met up with Father."

Marie is silent on the other side. Her soft breathing is the only way to acknowledge her presence.

"He's doing all right. Wanted to send me home, though."

Marie hums softly, shuffling around. Jaamini listens to the rustle of her mother's dress, the sound of the leaves under her boots, the sway of trees and birds faintly chirping.

"Do you miss it?" Marie asks.

"Miss what?" Jaamini counters. Her head drops on the back of the couch. A moment passes as her eyes close and she drifts back across the sea. "Yes," she croaks out.

"But you'd rather kill and steal with your father than live peacefully with your mother."

Jaamini pulls the phone from her ear and glares at it, knowing it won't change anything.

"No, Mother. I came here to do my duty."

"Duty! *Idiota*. My daughter has no duty to those people."

"Ma," Jaamini says.

"You shouldn't even be there. Your grandfather just died, and all you want to do is run," Marie hisses. The phone goes silent on her end, but she doesn't drop the call.

Jaamini bites her lip, her fingers curling into a fist. "Every one of us owes our lives to this gang. If not for them we would have died out a long time ago. If they request for us to serve under them for the rest of our lineage, then so be it," Jaamini says.

"I thought you were better than that. Forgive me, Mini, but . . . don't come home." The phone clicks when she hangs up.

Jaamini stares blankly into the darkness of the TV. Blood pools under her teeth and drips down her lip. Her fists shake in her lap.

"Hey, I'm—" Tony rushes to her side and quickly dabs at the tears sliding down her face. He gently pries at her chin. She eventually releases her abused lip from her teeth.

Her hazel eyes refocus with tears streaming down her face.

"Let's get you cleaned up, and then let's go."

Jaamini nods and allows Tony to take her to the kitchen sink to wash her face and clean her lip.

"Here," he says, fishing something blue from the kitchen

drawer. Jaamini takes the offered ball. It's a deep navy blue with light sparkles; it feels squishy and gel-like.

"Stress ball. It's Adelio's, but recently he hasn't needed it." Tony takes her forearm and gives a gentle tug. Jaamini frowns. Her eyes sparkle like a storm of stars.

"Thank you," she whispers. Tony doesn't respond. The two leave the apartment and head out to the parking lot.

CHAPTER 7

They get into Tony's car, and he pulls off quickly.

"I really like having you here," Tony says.

"I haven't been here that long," Jaamini mumbles, squeezing the sparkly stress ball. It bulges past her fingers but doesn't pop. She relaxes into her seat, never letting her grip up.

"Since you got here, Adelio's been all chipper, I don't have to make breakfast alone, and I don't have to drive Pinky around like an Uber. Now we're a group heading to the same place and not public transportation."

Jaamini laughs and rolls her shoulders. "I'm just as tense around him as you are," she confesses.

"Why?" Tony asks, glancing her way.

"My father has never been abusive, but he's definitely . . . *off.*" She sighs, and Tony grumbles.

"The Sanz men are all . . . strange. I mean, Sullivan has a tendency to shoot first, talk later. He has no sense of humanity in him."

"With his line of work, how could he?" Jaamini asks. Noticing how tense Tony got, she adds, "No offense to you, of course. You seem sweet."

He grins at that. "I owe it all to my crew. We used to be separate from them, but so much happened last year we got absorbed. Totally Adelio's fault."

Jaamini's hands relax. "Well Adelio does some interesting things himself."

"Yeah, that's why I'm nervous about getting a surrogate."

"Surrogate?" Jaamini asks, sitting up in her seat. Tony pulls the car over in front of a large house. The front door is more intimidating than anything. It's a strong oak door, nothing special, but her father is already standing in the doorway with his arms crossed.

"We can talk about this later, but I have a question."

Pinky closes and locks his front door. His steps are slow and purposeful, thudding on the gravel walkway.

"What's Pinky's name?" Tony asks quickly.

"Name?" Jaamini asks.

"His real name—" Tony stops talking once Pinky reaches earshot. Jaamini blinks slowly, looking into her father's black shades. They're tinted so dark she can't see the outline of his eyes.

His leather jacket rustles under the cold November air. He looks at the two of them for so long that she starts to back into the door, her hand hovering over the handle.

Pinky grins, flashing his grill before he pops open the back door and gets inside.

"Tony, Tony, Tony," he says with a tsk. "Why so curious?" He throws his arms behind his head and smugly folds into his seat. Jaamini pinches her lips together and steals a glance Tony's way.

His shoulders are raised and tight. His hands flick at the gears. He tears off into the street without responding.

"I see," Pinky mumbles before shaking his head and chuckling. "Good morning, Jaamini," he says. Jaamini looks back at Tony once more.

"Good morning, Dad."

The air starts to warm. Pinky relaxes and snaps himself into his seat belt.

"Have you spoken to Marie?" he asks. Jaamini shrugs, turning her eyes to the window. She's looking, but her eyes can't catch anything as they zoom through the streets.

They finally slow in front of a house along a large strip of commercial buildings. A few residential places are scattered and speckled along the line.

"This is it," Tony says, but mostly for himself than for anyone else in the car.

The three of them get out of the car and walk up to the fence. Tony unlocks it with his key and swings the metal gate open for them.

They head up the stone walkway to the porch steps. Jaamini halts when the wind rustles two low-hanging wind chimes. She stares until a warm hand taps her.

Jaamini snatches her father's forearm before catching his gaze.

He grins and pulls her along.

"Sorry," she mumbles. The rush of her blood ebbs away. They enter the small house and step into a living room. It stretches from one wall to the other. A long couch wraps around a circular coffee table in the middle.

Pinky steps in front of them.

"I'm heading upstairs. Tony, watch over Mini for me."

Tony nods curtly. Pinky disappears into a corridor to their right, leaving behind only the sound of his feet ascending the steps.

"This is the armory, for lack of a better word," Tony

mumbles. He runs a finger over the end table and picks it back up, gray and dusty. He shakes his head in pity, then beelines through the living room to an archway into the hall.

Jaamini's head whips from one wall to the other as she looks at all the pictures of the gang members hanging out on the porch or at a pool. Some of them were on the beach and somewhere surrounded by drugs, booze, and money. Jaamini blanches at a man standing in front of a wall of bricks.

"Shouldn't they be more careful with the pictures they take?" Jaamini asks. She halts in the hall when she spots Sullivan lazing against the doorway with his arms folded over his chest.

He raises a dark brow.

"Problem?" he asks. His Spanish accent is much more prominent in the morning. He smiles and waves them over.

"No problem with me. I just think if the cops got a warrant, all your secrets can be read over the walls," Jaamini answers. Sullivan chuckles and walks through the office to the chair on the other side.

She shakes her head at the irony.

All the big bosses must have an office.

Tony stands by the door while she takes a seat on the other side of the desk.

"So, Mini, welcome to America. I suppose the voyage wasn't hard?"

She shakes her head. "No. I've been to America before. I was just really young."

Sullivan nods his head of graying curls. They swoop around his forehead freely. "What business do you bring?"

Jaamini sits straighter in her seat, tucking her phone and stress ball away into the hidden pockets in her dress.

"I've come to claim my birthright," she says. Her voice comes out louder and harsher than she intended. Sullivan reaches across the table and snatches up a feather pen.

"Why exactly should I allow that?" he asks, and she can hear the accusation in his tone.

"I am not asking you to go against my father's wishes, but I am asking for you to allow me to do what every Reyes before me has done. For the debt we owe to you," she says.

Sullivan sighs and pulls a piece of old yellowing paper from his desk.

"You see this?" He slides the paper over to Jaamini. She lifts to the front of her chair. Her hair blocks off the sides of the paper from anyone else as it gently sweeps down the paper's length.

"Yes, I see it," she says.

At the top of the contract are the words, "Kill Switch Operator."

"I'll let you join if you agree to these terms."

Jaamini stares at the contract for a long time, her brows furrowed. She glazes over it.

"You don't—" he starts, but she holds out a finger, a lost determination resurfacing in her eyes. He uses the tip of the feather to prick her finger. Blood collects at the top of her skin.

Jaamini gingerly plucks the feather from his hand and signs in one fluid swoop at the bottom of the page.

Sullivan passes over a wipe, and she cleans off the feather and her finger. He hands her a Band-Aid, and she gratefully takes it.

"Welcome to the family, dear Mini."

She takes his hand and shakes it. His gaze changes from leveled and cold to soft and warm.

"It's good to have a Reyes back in the gang."

She smiles, though it doesn't reach her eyes. "I am sure my ancestors are smiling," she says.

He chuckles and takes the slip. He stands and straightens out his suit jacket. His amber dress shoes tap lightly at the hardwood floor.

Tony joins her, sitting in a chair. His eyes show it all, the worry that she just signed her soul away. Her shoulders sink.

I did.

"I will be fine," she mouths. Tony rolls his baby blues and reaches for her injured finger. He makes one of those motherly faces, and she grins.

"Here." Sullivan slides a copy of her contract over to her, and Tony's mouth drops open. His eyes go wide. His hands shake while he pulls it closer. Jaamini leans away from him. Tony looks about ready to vomit.

His eyes flicker from the paper to Sullivan, then to her. "Why?" he asks softly.

Jaamini stands, taking the paper and rolling it up. She pulls a strand of string from her dress and ties the paper like a scroll. It's very reminiscent of her father's behavior.

"It's my duty to serve regardless of the job given," Jaamini deadpans.

"Glad you feel that way," Sullivan says. His deep brown eyes sparkle with merit. Tony stands up abruptly, knocking his chair back.

"Right. Duty."

Jaamini stands stiffly at his tone. He sounds just like her mother. She shakes her head. "Come on," she says. Tony reluctantly lets her drag him out of the office.

"Later, Boss," she calls.

"You can still call me Uncle. Boss is putrid," Sullivan calls back.

"Later, Uncle."

He nods. Tony storms through the house to her father. She follows, light on her feet.

Tony jumps up the stairs, taking them three at a time. Jaamini sighs and climbs them at a sluggish pace, restricted by her dress.

CHAPTER 8

Jaamini stops walking when she reaches the room Tony sped inside.

A group of young women sit in the corner talking. One girl's hand is in her purse and visibly twitches. Her fur vest isn't much to cover the lingerie she's resting in. Her eyes flick to Jaamini, and she rolls them.

"Aren't there enough of us?" the woman asks. Tony looks back at Jaamini.

"She's not here for that. She's one of us."

The girl's mouth pops open, and all the women turn to Jaamini. Their gazes are bright and intense. They look her over. Jaamini squares her shoulders.

"Don't look at me like that. It's demeaning," Jaamini says. One of the girls opens her mouth to talk, but Pinky puts the barrel of his gun on her temple.

"You heard her," he growls.

I had it covered. It's not like they would do anything. Jaamini keeps her complaints to herself. She can tell by the way the rest of the women flinch that they may have guns but don't favor one held at them. She frowns when her father hesitates to remove his gun. Pinky sighs, stuffing it away into his concealed holster.

"Tony," Pinky calls, shuffling through some of the files in the cabinet. Tony pops over to his side, and they discuss something in hushed whispers.

Jaamini takes a seat on the far side of the room and admires the tall bookshelves that line the walls. One of the girls pops over to her and crosses her legs. Her pleated skirt hikes up, but she doesn't dare try to fix it.

"You're Pinky's daughter, right?" she asks. Her warm brown eyes lock Jaamini in place with a blank stare.

"Yes. I'm Jaamini. You?"

"I'm Sey, the resident Asian."

Jaamini shakes her hand. "How's that part important? No offense."

Sey snickers. "Most of the people here are Latina or Spanish. I may speak Spanish, but I am definitely not. So I introduce myself as Asian," she says.

As if having broken a wall in her mind, Jaamini swoops her eyes around the group in wonder. Her father isn't fully Spanish, and Tony doesn't seem to be Spanish either, but low and behold, all the women she sits across from are.

"Do I not look Spanish?" Jaamini asks, turning back to Sey. The woman is thumbing through a magazine without a modicum of interest.

"You just look comforting. I remember being your age—thought I could run the world," Sey says. Her eyes slowly lift from the page, and she gives a lopsided smile. "I'm sure with guidance you'll do much better than me," she adds.

Jaamini looks down at her hands sitting idle in her lap. Her nails have grown long—long enough to scratch someone's eyes out. Every time she blinks, she can see it. The russet color of blood. The coppery smell.

Guidance won't fix any mistakes she makes from now on.

"Are you offering?" Jaamini asks. Sey stops aimlessly flipping and throws the magazine on the end table by her armrest.

"No. I am the last person you want teaching you anything," she says with a shrug. "I couldn't even get the guy I wanted," Sey whispers.

Tony whips around, a frown marring his fair skin. "It's not my fault. I apologized," Tony says quickly.

"I know," Sey says cheerily and leans her head on the back of the couch. Jaamini's mouth drops open.

"Ew. You wanted to be with Big Cuz?"

All the women in the room turn to her, questions on their lips.

"How is Adelio your cousin?" Sey asks.

Their family tree is pretty complicated, but she should be able to simplify it . . . somehow.

"The easiest way to explain is we aren't blood relatives, but our families are tightly knit."

Sey leans in rather close, a sweet, tangy scent wafting from her person. "So you understand the sentiment that Adelio is hot," she whispers. Jaamini cringes back, frantically shaking her head.

"No, I do not understand the *sentiment*." Jaamini's whispered hiss is enough to get Tony's attention. He stands in front of them with his arms crossed.

"Stop bothering her. Go do something."

Sey stands up. Her short legs put her up to his solar plexus. Sey's glare radiates from behind her body and she stands tensely.

"All right, Boss," she says in a sticky-sweet voice, then slinks out of the room. Jaamini looks between them. Tony is unfazed.

"Sorry about her. She's still upset about something that happened a long time ago."

Jaamini stands up and stretches. "It's okay. I don't really mind."

Tony's phone beeps, and he pulls it out. His regular calm face molds into a silent rage.

"Pink, I gotta go."

Pink? Jaamini almost bursts out laughing. *Pinky is already a nickname. Who shortens a nickname? Does he really not know his name?* Jaamini misses half the conversation, tuning back in to catch the last breath.

". . . with you," Pinky says. Tony's shoulders sink, and he runs a hand through his hair.

"Fine, then you two can get an early lunch or something. I just really have to go."

"It's on your pocket," Pinky says, dropping the stack of manila folders. He leaves everything where it is and flicks his gaze at the group of women. They flinch and keep their heads down.

As much as Jaamini wants to believe they're dressed how they are because they like to be, she's getting a horrible sinking feeling in her gut that they're not.

"Come on, Mini," Pinky calls after her. One of the women glares into Jaamini's pity-filled eyes. They leave the house in haste.

Jaamini tries to catch up with her zooming counterparts. Pinky opens the door for her and helps her up before jumping into the back. Her seat belt is barely on before they are pulling off in the opposite direction of which they came.

"Not to bother, but where are we going?" she asks.

"My restaurant," Tony says.

"You own a restaurant?" Jaamini asks, readjusting her skirt and feeling around her pockets to make sure she didn't leave anything.

"Yes. Adelio and I opened it a year ago on our anniversary of getting back together."

Jaamini nods, a smile hidden behind her hair. Her cousin is such a sap! The tires screech as they pull into the employee parking zone.

Tony jumps out and holds the back door open to them. They amble inside, and he directs a host to them.

The blond hostess bounces over to them on the balls of her feet. Her eyes sparkle behind shiny glasses.

They follow her out onto the restaurant floor and to a seat in the back not far from the kitchen door.

"I will call your waiter over now. Excuse me." She rushes off to the other side of the restaurant and halts someone on their feet. Jaamini looks to her father, who rubs at the bridge of his nose and scrunches his face.

"I took a position," she blurts. He halts and pushes his shades back up his face.

"What are you talking about?" he asks softly. His shoulders are slumped, and he sinks down in his seat like he's never getting back up.

"I talked to Sullivan about joining—"

Pinky holds up a hand as footsteps lightly fill the air around them. Jaamini sighs, sweeping her gaze over to the waiter.

Her eyes widen as she takes him in.

His rich brown skin glows under the low yellow light, a harsh gold radiating around him. His eyes catch her attention, so much deeper and sharper than Tony's. They're a numbing blue like her mother's favorite gem, zircon.

Jaamini stares at him, her mouth slightly ajar. Pinky eyes her and sighs.

"Hi, I'm Tor. I will be your server today. What can I get

you?"

Jaamini sucks in her breath sharply and returns her gaze to the menu. "Is it too early for pasta?" she asks quickly, her cheeks warming.

"Nope. Would you like a specific type?" he asks.

She risks looking up at him. He wears a light smirk, and her face warms more as she thumbs through the menu.

"I'll have the spicy red chicken alfredo with a strawberry sundae," she mumbles.

"It's very hot. Are you sure?"

She nods, ignoring the tingles his smoky voice causes to wash over her. Pinky waits to order long enough for her to catch his gaze. It's guarded, dark, and unreadable.

"The same for me, and while you're at it, coffee . . . black."

"Yes, sir. I will be right back."

The two stay quiet until Tor is out of earshot.

"Like I was saying, I'm in now," Jaamini continues.

Pinky frowns. He watches her closely. He has yet to move from his spot, but his eyes flicker so frantically behind his shades she can see them moving.

"Which contract?"

Jaamini hesitates, wishing she could wash her dry throat away with her strawberry sundae.

"Kill—"

He holds his hand up again, cutting her off. He rights himself in his seat. His shades slip down the bridge of his nose, and he peers into her eyes.

"Are you f—are you kidding me?" His hushed whisper is sharp and pronounced. She backs away, aware his accent slipping is never a good thing. Folding her arms over her chest, she raises her chin to him.

"I'm sixteen and the smartest protege in the Reyes family

of four generations. I know what I'm doing."

Their gazes don't level until three cups are placed in front of them. Two are large glasses full of strawberry sundaes, and the other is a white mug full of steaming coffee.

"Excuse me," Tor mutters lightly, grasping the menus. "Is there anything I can get you now before I grab your food?" he asks. His blue eyes flicker from Jaamini to Pinky. With a sigh, he steps slowly toward the kitchen.

CHAPTER 9

Jaamini leans back in her chair.

"I'm sorry," she mumbles. Pinky sips at his coffee.

"You think you understand the game because you've been trained. Training your combat skill and honing your tactile thinking is not anything like being on the field. It's nothing like taking a life."

Jaamini picks at her sundae, shivering slightly.

Pinky strips off his leather jacket and holds it out to her. She takes it gingerly and zips herself up.

"Hey," Tony says, popping up at their side. "Your food's almost out. I have a few more things to do, so text me when you're done, and I will be on my way out."

Pinky nods, a frown etched into his face. Tony stares for a second.

"Is there anything I can do to ease this disgusting amount of tension?" Tony asks.

"Shut up," Pinky snarls. Tony rolls his eyes and pats Jaamini's shoulder before disappearing into the back. Tor rolls a tray over and sets their pasta down.

"If you need a refill or anything else, just let me know."

Jaamini smiles in thanks and quickly picks up her fork.

"Can you bring us hot water and lemons?" Pinky asks.

"Yes, sir. Be right back."

Jaamini looks at her dad with a raised brow. "This is Tony's place. You think he would let the dishes out without cleaning them?"

"Shush. Not talking to you right now," he mumbles and wrings his hands out. His eyes are lost somewhere beyond her shoulder.

Jaamini rests her face on her hand and continues to sip at her sundae until the water arrives.

Once they clean their utensils, they both sit in silence. Jaamini tries talking to Pinky twice, but he keeps his sour face.

Toward the end of her meal, her phone buzzes, saving her from his never-ending cold shoulder. Jaamini's eyes scan the text. Her brows knit together.

"I guess your new job's already been approved. It's time to meet the crew."

"Oh . . . that was pretty fast," Jaamini mumbles.

"Life is short," Pinky says.

"It happened like thirty minutes ago."

Pinky flicks his watch, and the screen lights up. "It's been an hour. Hurry up so we aren't late."

Jaamini glares at him but listens to what he says, finishing her plate before he does. Tony joins them at the back door, and they head out to his car.

"So what's this about? I didn't get a text," Tony says.

"Wasn't for you," Pinky says under his breath. He keeps his eyes out the window.

"Oh, for goodness sake! Are you seriously sulking right now?" Tony asks incredulously. Pinky doesn't respond, and Jaamini plays with her new stress ball.

Tony mumbles some very insulting phrases about adolescents under his breath. If her father cared enough, that surely would have gotten the man killed.

Jaamini holds her breath as they walk up to the door. She isn't exactly dressed to make a strong impression, but this will have to do.

With her hands stashed away in her pockets, she steps through the front door into the darkened living room. The room is silent apart from one person typing away.

Sullivan leans against the wall, embracing his wife. They share glazed expressions. They smile when they see her.

"Hello, Niece!" Helena shrieks, skipping across the floor like a child. She gathers Jaamini into an embrace and kisses her forehead.

Jaamini allows herself to be pulled along to the front of the room.

"These are the Right Hands, all your aunties and uncles." Helena waves around the room. It's just her, Sullivan, Uncle Rio, and her father.

"Way to keep it in the family," Jaamini says with a chuckle, and the tension in her shoulders releases.

"Did you expect a giant man with an axe on his back, or a whole bunch of people in masks?" Helena asks, gleaming.

Jaamini shakes her head. "Your imagination is as wild as ever, Auntie," she says.

"Now that you're all here, let's begin," Sullivan says. "Ah, yes. Tony, retrieve Adelio from upstairs. Thank you."

Tony nods and departs for the stairs. His steps get lighter the farther into the house he walks.

Jaamini takes a seat on the couch next to her aunt.

"As we all know who Mini is, it serves no purpose to introduce her. But I will now pronounce her our new operator."

Rio's head snaps toward her, his multicolored eyes wide in shock.

"Mini can't be the operator," Rio says.

Sullivan raises a brow. "Why not?"

"Because that's ridiculous," Adelio says, stepping into the room. His arms fold tightly over his exposed chest. His flowery button-down shirt flows around his lean silhouette.

Sey's words from earlier creep into her head, and she almost gags in reflex.

"What's so ridiculous, Cousin?" Jaamini asks. His brown eyes flicker over to her, and he hesitates.

"You'll have to kill without hesitation. Women, children, the sick, the old. Can you do that?" he asks. His gaze is hard and caring, but behind it is a shimmer of worry.

"I can," she says, head held up.

"Good. Then to prove yourself, this is your target." Sullivan turns the TV on, and a man flashes on the screen. His bright yellow hair sticks out from under his hoodie, his hands stuffed deep into his pockets.

He isn't truly facing the camera, but she can clearly see the defining bump on the bridge of his nose.

"Deadline?" she asks, standing.

Sullivan grins. "Tomorrow, eleven p.m."

"Name?"

"Carter Jones."

"Sulliv—" Adelio starts.

"Let's see how she does," Sullivan says, cutting him off. Jaamini nods at Sullivan and turns sorry eyes over to Adelio.

Adelio's knuckles are white, and his eyes lose their shine. He glares at his father. Jaamini can see a faint red line trickling from his palm. Maybe he needs the stress ball after all.

Jaamini reaches for his hand and slips the ball into his palm, prying his fingers out of his flesh.

Adelio takes the ball and flexes his fingers over it. His gaze breaks, and he looks down into his hand.

"Father?" Jaamini turns to Pinky with a sweet smile. He raises a pink brow over his shades. "Gun," she says, holding her hand out. He stands, taking his gun from its holster.

Jaamini lifts her dress up to her lower thigh and switches her knife out for the gun. She passes the knife to him, and he stares down at its emblem for a long time.

"All righty." She leaves for the door without any further instruction.

"He was last seen at the gas station," Tony mumbles in the doorway.

"Cool. Thanks, Tony." Jaamini frowns at his downcast eyes. His shoulders are hunched. He stares holes into the porch.

Her gut twists, and bile surfaces at the back of her throat.

"You know him?" she asks, praying he says no. But his twinkling sapphires are the only answer she needs.

"Mini," Sullivan calls. She looks to her uncle. "Sey's going to take you." The man's shit-eating grin spreads across his face like a wildfire. The look in his deep brown eyes is wicked.

This is so wrong . . .

Sey joins her at the end of the porch. Even *her* dark eyes are blazing.

This man has to be a gang member, which means she can't just kill and run. It might be too personal.

The two of them get into a red Toyota parked in the driveway.

Sey fixes her flat purple bob and rubs red gloss over her already-ruby lips. Once she's ready, she fits her seat belt over her pressed burgundy pantsuit.

"I will take you to him, but that's all," Sey deadpans.

"Thank you," she whispers under her breath. Jaamini refuses to try understanding the situation. They pull out of the driveway and turn toward the inner city. The drive is through a familiar street, passing Tony's restaurant. The closer they get to the gas station sign in the distance, her heart beats faster.

Sweat breaks out around her neckline. Jaamini flexes her fingers and holds her hands together tightly. Her breathing is ragged.

Even her vision blurs in and out before she realizes she's crying. She dabs at her eyes until they're dry, and her throat cracks for water. Sey pulls up to the gas station.

"It's never too late to back out," Sey says. Jaamini looks at Sey's concerned face. She shakes her head.

"If I back out now, I dishonor my family name."

Sey rolls her eyes. Her knuckles go white over the leather steering wheel, and it creaks under her grip.

"He's my friend, Jaamini. He's family to me."

With shaking hands, Jaamini climbs out of the car and silently closes the door. Sey's eyes are rimmed in red, and tears threaten to spill. Jaamini turns away before they leave her eyes.

Her nails sink into her palm. She's just as bad as Adelio.

"Just find him," she whispers to herself and speeds into the gas station. Her eyes sweep over the people in the store. One man is dressed in all black. She trails through the aisles until she sees him making a coffee.

Her shoulders relax, and she lets go of the tension in her body. Her heeled flats click against the floor. Her hair whips off her shoulders with her speed. He turns to her, sharply ducking out of the way as she reaches forward.

CHAPTER 10

"You scared me there." Carter chuckles, setting his large cup down and opening a sugar pack. Jaamini looks him in the face. He smiles kindly, so she smiles back. His shoulders relax.

"Sorry, my sister's in the car. She said to hurry up," Jaamini lies. He chuckles dryly.

"Yeah, my sister is a pain as well. Are you new around here? Feel like I haven't seen your face."

Jaamini turns to him with a playful smirk. "Why? Interested?"

He chuckles a little too loud, running a hand through his shaggy blond hair. He knocks back his hood. "Nah. You're like twelve," he says, eyeing the creamer.

"Sixteen."

"Way too young," he mumbles. Jaamini shrugs, pouring hot water into her cup. "Coffee's over here."

"I don't drink coffee," she says, letting her hazel eyes run up and down his frame. He shuffles his feet. His hands drum awkwardly without rhythm on the counter.

"Do I know you?" he asks.

"No," she says, dropping a tea bag into her cup. His eyes widen at her curt response. He picks up his cup and takes another sip.

"I swear I've seen your face."

Jaamini shrugs, reaching into her pocket and pulling out her phone. He flinches back with lowered eyes.

"Well, it was nice to meet you," Carter says.

"Nice to meet me? You don't know my name."

He looks at her again and shakes his head, turning to leave.

"You forgot your cap," she says, twisting one in her hand. He looks down at his steaming cup and reaches for it. His eyes lock with hers officially, and his hand drops. With his mouth agape, he stares at her.

"Oh, wow . . . you look just like my boss," he whispers. She smiles genuinely. Jaamini is glad at least some people can recognize that she's his daughter.

"I'm gonna take that as a compliment."

He sputters, taking the cap and placing it gently over his sloshing coffee. "Oh, yeah, sorry. He's a handsome fella. I mean, well, never mind."

Jaamini raises a brow and flings her tea bag into the trash can. She pops a lid on her cup and leans against the counter.

"Sorry," he says again, running a hand through his hair.

"No problem." She adjusts her skirt and smiles. Jaamini's gun flashes against her thigh. Carter startles, backing away. She approaches him slowly. Oddly enough, her heart isn't thumping wildly in her chest.

Jaamini grazes past him.

Carter reaches toward his own holster, watching her warily. Jaamini stops at the counter and pays for her tea, aware he's watching her. She still has half a day and a very good idea of how to do this.

Jaamini leaves, reaching the car in seconds. Sey nibbles at her lips, ruining her perfect layer of gloss.

"He's not dead." Jaamini refrains from saying *yet*. "Let's go."

Sey nods slowly. The two of them watch as Carter pays for his half-empty coffee and pulls his hood back up.

He steps out and to the first pump. His eyes scan the area, not lingering long on their car until he sees Sey.

"See?" Jaamini says, sipping at her ginger tea.

"So, you won't do it?" Sey asks. Her voice cracks. Jaamini straps herself in and doesn't answer. Gulping, Sey pulls away from the gas station.

"Are you heading to the armory?" Sey asks, changing the topic.

"Take me to Tony's house," Jaamini says.

Jaamini texts Tony, and he replies instantly.

I'm stopping by.

See you soon.

When she gets there, she jumps out of the car quickly to dispose of her unsweetened tea and walks up to Tony. His eyes don't reach her.

"I haven't done it yet," she assures him. He looks up with a sigh.

"I really don't feel good about this," Tony says.

"Sullivan asked for it. You should take that up with him."

Tony frowns and rolls his shoulders. "You sound like Rio," Tony grumbles.

"He *is* my uncle."

Tony points toward the door and gives a quick wave to Sey. Sey beeps and peels off the sidewalk and into the street. When they get inside, Tony slams the door and starts pacing.

"He . . ." Tony mumbles, his voice fading. Adelio emerges from the inside of the house, looking Jaamini and Tony up and down.

"You did it?"

She shakes her head no. Sullivan stands up from the couch.

"When the hell did you get here?" she yelps.

"Been here the whole time. I just wanted to see how you operate. You've passed," Sullivan says.

Her head cocks to the side. His dark eyes dazzle in awe. He walks over to her with his arms outstretched in demonstration.

"You see, it was never about killing him. It was about your headspace: how quickly you comply, if you would do it regardless of who wanted you not to. It's all about mentality. This . . . *this* is the Kill Switch."

He laughs softly, making chills run down Jaamini's back.

"Even the most humane can become a murder bird." His shiny teeth gleam in the natural light. "Let's get Carter here and see how he feels about having been today's target. Hmm?" Sullivan turns to his son and straightens his suit jacket, the silken material swishing with his every movement.

Adelio takes out his phone, glaring the entire time. He turns to walk into the hall, Sullivan following him closely like a kid at a candy store. As soon as the two of them are out of sight, Tony pulls Jaamini into a hug.

"I don't care if you truly intended to kill him. Thank you for not doing it yet."

Jaamini frowns and pulls away. "I thought the operator had to be ruthless. What's Sullivan playing at?" she asks in a whisper. She checks around Tony's body to make sure the man himself is not present.

"It was never about killing; it's about molding the

human mind. But the nickname . . . that's going to stick," Tony explains.

"Nickname?" Jaamini asks.

"Murder Bird. If it weren't so grotesque, I would probably like it as well."

Jaamini takes a seat, holding on to her chest. Her vision blinks in and out.

"I was about to do it." She chuckles, putting her head back. "You know, she cried . . ." Jaamini says. Tony sits down next to Jaamini, resting his head back on the couch as well.

"Yeah, Sey and Carter go way back. She knew him even before he joined our old gang. But . . . yeah."

"What old gang?" She turns to Tony. He plays with the ends of his hair.

"We used to run a gang called Pistol Boys. In the last few years we were getting into big trouble. Bit off more than we could handle because we had a good amount of property and weaponry. Got too cocky and got consumed by Sullivan."

Jaamini hums, stretching out her limbs. Her fingers are going numb, and her chest is tight.

"Don't feel well," she mumbles. Breathing becomes harder. Her body gets warm. She blinks slowly. Tony says something, his voice soft and muffled. She gasps, holding her heart, her breathing stuttering.

Tony's hands grip her tightly, his voice booming and quiet all at once. Jaamini shakes her head, trying to fight the darkness edging around her vision. Footsteps pound through the hall until they fade out entirely.

*****

Jaamini's fingers twitch, and her head rings lightly. She squeezes her eyes. One of her hands is warmer than the other. The vision behind her eyelids is dark and cold like she's underwater. She tries resurfacing. Her arms thrash in front of her.

Her hands shake, getting colder and colder as she sinks under the pressure of her own mind.

*****

Jaamini opens her eyes to a dark room. Her hands are stuffed in fuzzy gloves. Her body is heavy and warm. She turns her head to both sides, looking over the peach and white tiles. The monitor by her side beeps in intervals.

Jaamini swallows until her mouth is dry. Pinky stirs in his sleep but doesn't wake up. Jaamini looks to her other side where Adelio rests his head on a small travel-size pillow.

"Oh, you're up."

Jaamini looks very slowly to the front where Carter stands.

One of his hands rests in his pocket, and the other holds a small cup of water.

"Let me get the doctor," he says before she can say anything. She coughs and scrunches her face in discomfort. Pinky sits up and rights his shades.

"Oh, you're up. You stupid—" He groans and pinches the bridge of his nose.

The doctor comes in quickly. She smiles gently, but it's not genuine. "Water?" she asks.

Jaamini nods. The doctor climbs around Adelio and pushes a button on the side of her bed. The top starts to lift her into a sitting position. The doctor offers a cup, and Jaamini reaches for it.

"You need to eat more and take your pills. That has some of your dissolved prescription in it."

Jaamini gulps it down despite the starchy pill taste swimming through her mouth. Her tongue swishes the cold liquid around.

She inhales the water before passing it back to the doctor.

"You're gonna prescribe me?"

The woman nods sharply. Her white hair is pulled into a tight bun at the nape of her neck. She grasps at reading glasses strung on a beaded gold necklace, then pushes them up her nose with a set of identical gold nails.

"You have a congenital heart defect, and it caused you to develop Long QT syndrome. That is why you fainted, and it *can* be life-threatening." She flits her eyes up to Jaamini before reading through the chart.

CHAPTER 11

"Have you been feeling well lately?" the doctor asks. Jaamini's heart monitor picks up. Her father's gaze burns into her cheek.

"Absolutely," she lies, and her heart skips. She turns to the monitor sheepishly. Pinky glares at the doctor.

"Making her feel some type of way. Shoo," he grumbles. The doctor looks at him like she wants to flip him the bird.

"No . . . impulses?" the doctor continues. Jaamini's stomach flips at her tone—her *accusatory* tone, the way the words fall from her lips and sink into Jaamini's skin like acid. Her heart starts hammering in her chest. Sweat collects around her neckline.

"I'm fine," Jaamini says. The doctor looks between her and the monitor. She takes off her glasses.

"All right. I will leave a recommendation with your father," the doctor says.

"I don't need a shrink," Jaamini says. The woman gives her a pitiful smile.

"Right, sweetie. You're stronger than that," she says curtly. Hate burns through Jaamini's blood, and her hands grip the sheets covering her legs.

When the doctor leaves, Jaamini lets out a hot breath.

"I'm gonna kill her before we leave," Pinky mumbles, leaning back in his seat. Jaamini nods, unable to think straight from the heavy fog clouding her heart.

"Not to pry, but why was she talking to you like that?" Carter asks.

"Suicide watch," Jaamini deadpans. Carter's teeth clack together as he quickly shuts his mouth.

Jaamini breathes deeply through her nose and hides her hands under her thighs. Her skin is itchy. Hot flashes rush up and down her body like hands.

Adelio's hand clasps hers, and he places a cold object in her hand. Jaamini grins when she feels the stress ball. She pulls her arms from under herself and stretches the ball until she can't.

"What time is it?" Jaamini asks.

"Eleven," Adelio says. She smiles sheepishly again.

"Heard you were out to get me." Carter chuckles. His large hands swallow the empty Dixie cup he holds.

"Yup." She keeps her eyes on the squishy blue blob creature she's making with the ball.

"Knew it," he says.

She finally looks at him. The smug look on his face is priceless.

"Was it obvious?" she asks humorously. Jaamini tosses the ball around nonchalantly, but her squared shoulders give her away.

"Well, you did flash your gun. I wasn't aware of how quickly you could have ended things until then."

"I wouldn't have," she says. Her voice goes higher in pitch. Carter wiggles his brown brows, which don't fit his sunflower-yellow hair.

"Sure. The nerve of kids these days." He scoffs and leans against the counter by the sink.

She chuckles and glances at her father. His folded arms give off an air of cockiness, but seconds later a light snore slips from his lips.

"This is the first time I have ever seen that man so relaxed. Who knew he had a kid?" Carter says with a light smirk.

Jaamini frowns. *Why didn't he tell anyone about my existence? Why aren't I his first topic of conversation? I'm his kid!*

"You should get some sleep. Visiting hours are over, so I'm heading home. Sleep well, Jaamini. See you around," Carter says.

"Bye," she responds with a nod, relaxing in her sitting position. She's not propped up well enough to stay awake without stimulation. The beep of her heart monitor lulls her to sleep.

*****

Jaamini yawns awake. She groggily listens as the morning doctor mumbles softly about taking her pills every day with a meal, then about how she needs to take one morning vitamin and a night vitamin.

Jaamini yawns throughout the whole thing, trying but failing to cover it with her arm.

Her doctor doesn't notice. Her eyes are glazed and puffy. Jaamini assumes it's from hours of crying.

The minute they step out of the hospital, they get into a sports car Jaamini doesn't recognize. Tony glares at Pinky.

Sitting in the back seat, Jaamini looks between her father's blank expression and Tony's pure hatred.

"You better have a good excuse," Tony says.

"I don't have to explain my actions to anyone," Pinky counters. Jaamini yawns into her arm again, looking at how tense Adelio is in the back seat next to her.

"What happened?" she asks in a whisper. She realizes she was louder than she thought when everyone looks her way. Tony rolls all the windows up and pulls out of the emergency entrance to the hospital.

"Your father took it upon himself to take more than a pinky early this morning."

"She hurt my little girl," Pinky says harshly. The car gets quiet and hot. Jaamini rolls down the window and sticks her head out.

"Oh . . . that. I didn't expect you to actually kill her," Jaamini mumbles.

"I didn't. Just . . . mutilated her."

Jaamini's head whips to the front where her dad grumbles.

"You tortured her?" She can barely see his shoulders rise and drop. "Dad," she says, dragging out the *a*.

"No, Mini. She deserved it. Just 'cause she thought it was your fault you were in the hospital didn't give her a right to treat you like that, or even look at you like she was better in any sort of way."

Jaamini leans forward in her seat, poking the back of his, knowing he can't feel it. "What did you take from her?" she grumbles.

"Nothing."

"An entire arm!" Tony says, voice rising with each syllable.

Adelio gently drags Jaamini's hand from the back of the seat and presses her back against her own seat.

"It's too late to change anything," he says in one breath and rolls his window down. His mouth is pulled into a pout, and his leg is bouncing.

Everyone in this car is crazy except for Tony. It seems even she falls under that insane category. Sighing loudly, she watches the birds outside soar high into the clouds.

*****

Pinky hauls Jaamini's sleeping body into the house. He places her down gently on the bed.

"I can walk, Dad," she mumbles sleepily.

"No. You need to take your vitamins and eat before I let you move. And once you finish eating you need to go to sleep before I let you get up." He nods, affirming himself.

"Why'd you separate—never mind, I don't care. Why do I have to be in here?" She motions around the penthouse room.

"I live here, and now so do you," Pinky says.

"I was supposed to be staying with Auntie," Jaamini whines, throwing her arms around like a kid.

"Nope."

"Why not?"

"You weren't taking your medicine."

"I forgot it . . ."

"Your fault then." He turns to the door and thinks better of it. Pinky places his hands on his hips and turns to her with that look.

She loathes that look.

"You better stay in that bed or I won't be nice anymore," Pinky says.

"Dad."

"No, Jaamini. I trusted you to make good decisions no matter where you were. But look where we're at."

He leaves the room. The door slams shut after his

stomping feet. Jaamini throws her arms up and lets them thump down against the sinking mattress.

Memory foam. She can feel her form molding into the surface. With a sigh, she reaches for her phone . . . which is missing.

Great.

The stress ball, on the other hand, is still in her pocket. She pulls at it, trying to break it from her absolute boredom.

*****

Jaamini wakes up on the floor. She peels her cheek off the cold wood and yawns. *I need to sleep in the middle of the bed next time.*

From her place on the floor she can she her phone under the bed. She grabs it quickly.

Jaamini rubs her sore jaw and straightens out her dress. She moves the blinds and peers out the window.

From the penthouse, she can see the hills where the Hollywood sign is. She smiles and pulls the blinds closed. When she turns back around, she finds her white suitcase placed against the wall.

It's empty except for her knife. She switches her father's gun out for her knife and opens the dresser adjacent to the twin-size bed.

All her underwear are folded perfectly. Her socks are bundled. She opens the next drawer, which is full of her neatly pressed jeans, shorts, and leggings. Under that are her shirts and dresses, all immaculately folded. Only her father would take time to fold everything.

She grabs leggings and one of her long-sleeved crop tops. She really doesn't want to let go of summer, but it's almost Thanksgiving. She's going to freeze to death if she keeps wearing summer dresses and not her sweater dresses. She only has three of those, and with her current *profession*, they do not seem practical.

CHAPTER 12

Jaamini startles Tony when she reaches the kitchen.

"No offense, but why are you here?" Jaamini asks him.

Tony laughs and points at Adelio lazing about, dead on the couch. At least he looks dead. His eyes are drooping, and his head nods every few seconds.

"He wanted to make sure you were okay. Plus, I like to be here by eight a.m." Tony smiles. Jaamini joins him at the kitchen counter, sitting in a little nook not noticeable when one first walks into the apartment.

"You're practically my stepmom at this point."

Tony halts and looks at her with a grin. "I am, aren't I? We never did finish our conversation."

Jaamini waits as Tony pours her some water and gets back to whisking eggs.

"Adelio and I have been married for a year and change now. It was a spur-of-the-moment kind of thing. We went to Vegas and just got hitched. Something stupid kids do, you know?"

"Stupid adults too," Jaamini mumbles, sipping at her glass.

"That too. Anyway, once everything was said and done, we decided we'd give marriage a try. We moved all his stuff down here, and that was it. Now I finally have the restaurant I wanted."

Jaamini places her half-empty glass down. "And now you want kids?" she asks quietly. Tony nods and pours the eggs into the pan. He snatches up his spatula and watches the crackling pan. The sweet heady oil scent drifts around them and through the apartment.

"While wealth is fleeting, family is forever. Since I have the means to have kids now, I want them."

"What if you always have the means, like for the rest of your life?"

He chuckles and flips half of the egg over, making a colorful peppered omelet.

"Then not only will I have the means, but I will also have a family. What do *you* want?" he asks over the sound of Adelio getting more comfortable on the couch.

Jaamini shrugs, reaching for the door to the fridge and pulling the water pitcher out.

"I just want to be proud of myself," she says.

They don't speak again until the plates are full of thick omelets and surrounded by grits and bacon. Pinky resurfaces from the middle of the apartment and makes his way over to eat.

He glares at Adelio while he simultaneously stuffs his face.

"You really don't like my cousin. What's that about?" Jaamini asks while Pinky clears the plates. He scoffs and rolls his shoulders.

"Pushing it off is only going to make me more curious. What did Adelio ever do to you?" she pries, pulling his sleeve. The fleece is soft and fluffy under her fingertips.

Pinky peels her grasp off his sleeve and takes her hands in his.

"Nothing. I am just spiteful," he mumbles.

Seeing a happy marriage every day must really be getting to him, she thinks, pulling a lock of hair behind her ear. Pinky sighs and gives her a tight hug.

"You need to report to the house. I am heading out for a bit, so Tony and that numbskull will watch over you while I'm gone."

"Where are you going?" Jaamini asks, following his receding steps toward the door. He grabs his keys and pops the creaky front door open. He grins at her and waves before departing down the hall toward the elevator.

"Where do you think he's going?" Jaamini asks, closing the door and waiting for Tony's response.

"Maybe he's heading in for a mission. I don't care much, and you shouldn't either," Tony says.

"But he's my dad."

Tony smiles softly. "I know."

Jaamini's phone buzzes in her hand, and she looks down at the unknown number.

Head to the house, and you will be met with your next mission.

Jaamini stares at the phone for a long minute before passing it to Tony.

"This is Sullivan's number. Your next official mission has just been assigned. I hate when I'm not briefed before arriving," Tony says. He rolls his eyes and hands her phone back. "Let's go. I'll drop you off and head to the restaurant."

Jaamini follows him. She takes one last look at her big cousin before joining Tony at the car. He jumps in, and they tear into the streets toward the armory.

Jaamini steps out of the car, smoothing her clothes and wringing her hands.

A small group relaxes against the fence, passing a bag full of candy around. Jaamini frowns at them. She straightens her back and holds her head up.

Tony gives a beep, and she waves goodbye. Her eyes catch on one guy in particular.

Electric-blue eyes hold her gaze for a moment too long before he turns his attention to the woman at his side.

"You remember Carter, right?" Sey asks with a gruff voice. Jaamini nods curtly, holding out a hand for him to shake.

"Hello again, Murder Bird," Carter says. She opens her mouth to object to the nickname, but she can't find the right words.

"Let's get this over with," Sey says.

"What are we doing?" Jaamini asks.

Sey folds her arms over her chest. "Someone will brief you on the ride over," she says, then motions to her small car and then another. "Who are you riding with?"

Jaamini eyes the white Volvo and Sey's red Toyota. "Does it matter?" she asks after silence creeps over the group.

"Yes, it matters. Never mind. Just come with me." Sey takes her hand rather forcefully and hauls her to the passenger door. "Listen, I don't hate you, okay? I'm just not over it."

Jaamini bites her tongue. She keeps down the response clawing up her throat. *I didn't ask,* she thinks to herself and gets into the stuffy car as soon as the door unlocks.

As cold as she is, it's still not cold enough to comfortably sit in the hot car.

"Grab the gun from the glove compartment," Sey says.

Jaamini pulls the compartment open and keeps her eyes out the windshield while reaching for it. Once she grabs ahold of the cool metal, she places it in her lap.

The dark blue plated revolver has small yellow stars across the plate and a silencer on the front. Jaamini checks the safety before twisting it around in her hand to admire the handiwork.

"Not much of a gun person," Jaamini says. Sey briefly looks at her and hides a smirk behind her pastel purple bop. She rolls the windows down a bit, the icy air ripping through the car at lightning speed.

"I wasn't much of one either once upon a time, but after I joined the Sanz it was practically a necessity. Someone always has a reason to shoot."

"Do you kill often?" Jaamini asks in a whisper. Sey doesn't respond.

They start driving slower as they pull into unfamiliar territory. Nowhere in front or behind them is the beach or even the penthouse, just rows and rows of houses.

"We're going to be in and out. Just buying tickets and meeting up with two other people. Then we get on a cruise, and the rest is bagging and tagging."

"We're robbing people?" Jaamini asks. Sey eyes her cautiously.

"You work for a gang leader with a house full of military grade weaponry. Yes, were robbing people. How else do you get things?" Sey asks.

Jaamini stares down at her hands and swallows the dry fear creeping through her chest.

"You've never stolen anything?" Sey asks. They slow down by a pier with small shops and a coffee shop lining the walkway.

Sey parks the car in the parking lot of the pier in front of a giant cruise ship. Jaamini gawks at its pristine white color and flashy design of waves on the side. Jaamini looks around and spots a sign reading, *"Marina del Rey."*

"We're getting on that?" Jaamini asks.

"Just for a bit. You and I are hitting up that house."

Jaamini marvels at the sheer size of the boat. They get out and approach the man retying a sailboat.

It is the only thing she can recognize among the expensive boats and dressy people. *It's too chilly for flashy clothes.*

She gapes as a woman walks by in a lightweight fur coat and seven-inch heels. Shaking her head, Jaamini tunes into the conversation.

"Yes, we are all getting on," Sey says.

"All right, six tickets it is. Just a minute." The man behind the ticket booth says.

Jaamini watches the horizon as boats glide through the water. The water is dark, swirling around the underside of the boat.

A man drives by and gives a nod to Sey, and she returns it, then graciously takes the tickets with a smile.

The two get back into Sey's car, and she waits a minute before turning it on.

"Everything is a go. Now to get dressed," Sey says.

"Dressed?" Jaamini asks.

"We're going to dinner, darling!" Sey says, smirking before clicking her seat belt into place and pulling off the way they came.

CHAPTER 13

Jaamini shuffles the tight cocktail dress around her narrow hips. Her lips turn down as she looks up at Sey's curves. The woman is effortlessly gorgeous in anything she wears, her purple bob fluttering around her ears and her skintight mermaid dress fanning out around her calves.

Sey's heels click against the concrete, and she meets arms with Carter. He smiles gently and loosens his tie. Jaamini puts her hands behind her back and walks silently until they arrive at the car with the two other members she's not met.

One of them has a bald head, pointed tips on his ears, and a Rolex. The men are dressed in all black.

How . . . charming.

Jaamini almost rolls her eyes until the waiter, Tor, steps into view. He's paired his black tux with a shimmery blue satin top.

His eyes stroke the length of her dress before he offers an arm. Jaamini clears her throat, taking it gingerly. A wash of herbal oils wafts into her nose.

"You just as nervous as me?" he asks. His eyes aren't on her, and his voice is low. Jaamini nods, taking slow and steady breaths. She doesn't need any heart problems here.

He glances at her, the setting sun lighting up his eyes. Jaamini hurriedly lets her gaze wander up the torchlit pier.

Men and women talk softly to the people next to them. She glances behind them, surveying the faces. Most of them seem older, rich, and very well put together.

No wonder Sey grabbed the tightest dress in the history of the world. Jaamini unconsciously straightens her back and raises her gaze from the ground.

Tor snickers by her side, tugging her closer.

"You're too beautiful to have to fit anyone's standards. Just relax," he says. She clears her throat.

"You don't even know my name," Jaamini counters.

"Jaamini Reyes," he says. A smirk crosses his face.

"So, who are you?" she asks.

He hands the attendant their tickets, and they walk up the landing into the ship. Sey holds firmly to Carter's hand but lets go the instant Jaamini catches her gaze.

Noted.

"Let's go to our seats," Sey says. The six of them head past the docking area into the dining hall. They split into pairs and take their seats.

Jaamini's hand sits poised above the name on her card. Her brows furrow when Tor takes her hand and pulls her toward her chair.

She can feel her face heat up when he sits her down and pulls a rose from somewhere to hand to her. The orange rose's petals fade into a buttery yellow. The middle spreads into a deep russet.

"It's very pretty," Jaamini says.

"Thank you. It's . . . *handpicked*," he says.

She raises a brow at him, forcing away the smile tugging at her lips. "From where?" she asks, eyeing the center of the table. She tucks the rose into the vase before anyone can say anything. He leans in, elbows on the table, and stares at her. Jaamini tucks and pulls at her straightened hair.

Maybe I should have left it.

"You look less Spanish—" he starts.

"What can I get you?" the waitress asks. Her eyes lock on Tor.

Jaamini straightens in her seat and clears her throat. No way is she about to get ignored. Her stomach twists when the waitress's gold-brown eyes land on her.

"Yes?" the waitress drawls. Her voice is dry and lackluster.

"We'd like a minute if that's okay with you." Jaamini's hand gently clasps Tor's, twisting their fingers together. The waitress looks between their hands and Tor's face before stepping back with a wide, strained smile, then wanders off toward another table.

Jaamini keeps smiling until she disappears out of sight.

"You jealous, love?" Tor asks. His sparkling eyes shine like a light bulb. Jaamini pulls her hand back hastily.

"No . . . I was . . . whatever."

Tor just smiles and pulls their menus together. "We don't exactly have time to eat," he says.

"I know." Jaamini watches Carter and Sey throw half-lidded looks over the table. "You know anything about that?" she asks.

Tor turns and looks at the two of them. He shrugs and looks at her. "Apparently things got heated over the phone one day; it was recently though. He said something about being a target."

Whatever hunger stemmed from the smell of steamed food, warm bread, and caramel drinks is gone. Jaamini holds her stomach as it rolls painfully slowly.

"Judging by your face, I assume you already know that," he says. His eyes do a quick sweep of the area.

"Yeah, but it's not like I proved I could . . . I just proved I would . . . I think that's where it came from," Jaamini rambles.

"At least your nickname is cool. Mine is totally stupid."

Jaamini opens her mouth to ask, but the waitress comes back around with a grimace plastered over her face.

"What can I get for you?" she asks.

"Water," Jaamini says immediately. *To throw.* Jaamini keeps her mouth sealed shut, never taking her gaze from the woman's face. She needs to let it go, but this weird weight presses against her shoulders, and she balls her fists.

She doesn't even realize she was glaring until the waitress speeds away to get their drinks.

Tor breaks out into a laugh before Jaamini brings herself back to present time.

"Not funny," Jaamini sneers.

"Hilarious, actually. She was only being slightly rude."

"It's not about that."

His smile vanishes, and they hold eye contact. His blue eyes reflect all the shiny chandelier flecks in the same manner a kaleidoscope would.

"Let's go." He stands and pulls her chair out for her.

"What?" Jaamini asks. Her brows pull together.

"It's time."

Jaamini follows silently, looking around for their waitress. She hasn't apologized yet, not that she really wants to, but the poor thing grabbed drinks for two people who aren't there to receive them.

Four of them arrive on the deck in seconds with no one around to see them.

"Wait . . . where's the boat?" Jaamini asks. Her voice

cracks, regret seeping into her skin. Sey points to a little speedboat following the ship's side.

Jaamini's stomach drops, and she prays this isn't what they have in mind.

"Why . . ." She can't even formulate her words. She's the closest to the rail, but they have to be kidding her. *No way are we about to . . . jump down.*

An ugly orange life jacket is thrust into her hands. She frowns, suiting up, and waits for something . . . anything.

Jaamini looks from Tor to Sey with absolute dread. Her hands are plastered to the crisp white railing, her knuckles starting to rival it in color.

"Fine, I'll jump first. Just know that I won't be nice if you don't jump," Sey says. She inflates her life jacket before promptly climbing up to straddle the railing, then throws herself down into the water. She narrowly avoids the side of each boat and is immediately pulled out. Jaamini looks at Tor as he inflates his jacket.

Her hand shoots out to stop him.

"We don't have time, my love," he says.

Tor is off the boat in an instant, leaving Carter and Jaamini behind. A dark grin covers his face, and he flexes his fingers. Terror like no other runs up her back, and she inflates her jacket.

Don't scream. She takes a large inhale and climbs up on the railing. Her mind is reeling with possibilities as she pushes herself off. Her stomach drops to the water before her body. A silent scream rushes up her throat.

The moment her head fully submerges into the iceberg of a lake, two sets of hands haul her up and onto the deck. A warm towel is thrust into her arms.

Carter is the last to jump. He overshoots the boat. Jaamini holds back her gasp. She squeezes her hands into fists.

Carter's head pops out of the water, and he smirks at them. He wades until the boat pulls next to him, and Sey is able to haul him on deck.

The speedboat pulls away from the cruise ship's side, and they kick up water the faster they go. Jaamini grabs the closest stable thing—Tor. He snickers at her, flashing pretty white teeth.

"I thought you were new?" she whispers.

He shrugs. "I'm not new to taking risks if that's what you mean," he says.

Jaamini coughs, wiping her mouth. Her nose is burning, and she's shaking more than a chihuahua.

"Come on. We need to change," Sey says, pulling her deeper into the boat and down into a room where she passes her some baggy black clothes.

"Unfortunately for us, we don't have extra shoes."

"We can afford speedboats but no Nikes?" Jaamini rolls her eyes and strips down quickly to bundle up in the darkest apparel she has ever worn. All her personal clothes are an ash gray, not black.

Black is not her taste.

By the time they get out of the room, the boat is docking far into the distance from the ship. Jaamini can almost make out the ship she arrived on not two weeks ago.

Sey leads the way, and Jaamini follows, catching Carter's eye before she climbs into the car. He smiles at her before disappearing into his own unmarked vehicle.

The windows are so dark that the inside of the car can't be seen with the lights on.

Jaamini gets into the car and settles in next to Sey before Nico starts driving. He nods at her in the mirror, and she nods back.

CHAPTER 14

"When we get there, we'll head into the house up the street. We're parking a bit down the block, so put this on." Sey drops a masquerade mask, and a gun into her lap. The glittery gold mask has black decorative feathers sticking out the sides. Jaamini sighs and puts it on, fitting it to her face and pulling her dark hood over her hair. She looks like a mess—wedges, baggy tracksuit, and a shiny gala mask.

I look more suspicious in a masquerade mask than I do in a tight dress.

"Here we are," Nico says.

"Thanks." Jaamini steps down onto the street, thankful she's wearing wedges strapped around her ankles instead of some fancy heels. At least they stayed on her feet after a dive from the ship's height.

She shudders. *Never again.*

Jaamini follows Sey as they walk down the street.

"Whatever you do, don't take anything personal. It's just Viper stuff. I'm grabbing the information we came here for."

Jaamini nods. She's heard about the Vipers. They were just a bunch of rebellious Sanz members back when they were called the Serpents.

Whichever way she looks at it, they're just a bunch of snakes.

Jaamini's frown deepens as they walk between the two houses and toward the backyard. Both houses seem completely empty, pitch-dark, and silent.

Her heart squeezes. *Whose house is this?* Her gaze darts across the playground in the backyard, the rusty grill, and a few plastic chairs that sit around a table. It smells like barbecue and bubbles.

Strange how she can feel the house's presence. A chill rushes up her back. They climb the porch steps. None of the lights are on in the back either.

Sey pulls out a metal-plated card and places a gloved hand on the knob.

The door opens easily. Jaamini follows her in. Her heart hammers way harder than the short walk called for. She swallows dryly. Jaamini's wedges are muffled by the thick carpet.

Sey stops her, passing off a pair of gloves. Jaamini puts them on and takes the offered garbage bag.

Her eyes grow wary and heavy when she spots the serpent necklace framed on the wall. Sey walks past it, but she doesn't, slowly sliding it to the bottom of the bag. They creep around the downstairs through the living room, grabbing everything gold.

Why? She still doesn't know. Her arms get heavier every second even though her bag is practically still empty. Her heart aches when she passes the photo frames.

Three identical little girls smile while running toward the camera. Stubby little legs and tiny gaits. Her throat gets dryer the deeper into the house she goes.

She halts at the bottom of the steps, looking around for

Sey. With a deep sigh, she quietly ascends the stairs and steps into the first room—the bathroom.

Nothing catches her eye. Nothing but the light. *It's on.*

Her heart starts to race. She can't text Sey. She can't run around to find her. Whoever's here is collateral.

Licking her lips, she opens the next door. Her hazel eyes are met with toddler beds, each with a glittering pink canopy and a princess rug. Her stomach churns violently as she closes it.

It clicks quietly. Jaamini stills until no sound follows. Sey opens one of the doors, startling her. Both women lower their guns. Sey smirks and nods down the hall. Jaamini follows her to the last two doors.

Sey takes the door on the right and steps into the blackened room. Jaamini steps up to the other door. She hesitates.

A low amount of light, most likely from a lamp, pours under the door. With a steady hand, like she was taught, she opens the door.

A large man reaches for something in front of a dresser before thinking better of it. She steps into the room, her wedge clicking on the marble floor.

Jaamini jumps. The man turns toward the noise of her wedges. *Stupid womanly contraptions.* All the air leaves her in a whoosh. She reacts faster than she can think, her gun's recoil tossing her arm back. The pop is muffled. Jaamini steps back on unsteady feet as the man slowly reaches up toward his arm.

He hits the ground with a thump. Sey rushes to the room. The instant she sees him, a slew of curses leaves her mouth. Jaamini pushes the gun into its holster and moves out of her way.

Sey grabs the man, binding him and throwing his heavy

body to the bed. He gives out a shriek and looks up into her eyes fearfully.

"Where's the briefcase?" Sey demands. Her face draws in close to his, and her hair falls around him like leaves.

The man doesn't talk but stares. Sey pulls her own gun from her holster.

"Spill," she says, pressing the barrel to his neck.

"Fuck off," he growls past the tie in his mouth.

Sey raises her arm and gives him three quick lashes with her pistol.

Blood seeps through the tie and onto the bed. He grins up at her.

Sirens ring out in the distance. Jaamini moves around Sey and grabs the man by the throat. She pushes her gun into his mouth and pulls the trigger.

Blood splatters out, painting the white sheets red. She lets him go and fixes her gaze on Sey.

Sey leaves her side, looking around the room for the briefcase.

Jaamini avoids thinking about his body or even the soft whispers Sey makes into her phone.

Once she pushes everything into the bag, Jaamini turns back toward the bed. Blood soaks the sheets and spills onto the marble floor toward her heels.

Her lips turn downward. Jaamini steps back, the thick liquid sliding past her toward the end table.

"You got everything?" Sey mumbles, looking around. She points at something across the bed. With a bit of effort, Jaamini manages to pass the man's unmoving body to the dresser where she takes the large gold locket off the mannequin.

"Come on. We don't have much time now." Sey leaves in a hurry toward the front of the house, most likely to collect her bag. Jaamini stares down at the heavy man. He clings tightly to something in his pocket. His eyes remain open.

Jaamini holds her breath, stepping around the blood. Her legs are weak and heavy. Her arms are starting to shake. Her breathing comes short. The edges of her vision go in and out.

"Leave and take these. Straight down the street," Sey says, finding Jaamini where she left her.

Jaamini nods, unable to swallow with a desertlike dryness in the back of her throat. Sey sighs, stepping into the room with the man and closing the door.

Jaamini steps with a ferocity out of the house into the darkness of the night. Today's earlier ship jumping thrill is lost on her.

Icy air grazes past her, raising goose bumps on her skin. Her hair whips behind her in the wind. She turns her head left then right; no one is outside.

Jaamini walks stiffly down the street, straight to the trash cans at the end of the road.

Warm hands grasp her forearm. She jerks her arm away, breaking out of her stupor. Jaamini gasps, the first breath she has taken in minutes. The darkness around her covers the wild look in her hazel eyes.

"Don't know what happened, and I won't ask. Let's go." Tor hauls her down the street at top speed. Her arms ache from carrying the heavy bags, her feet hurt from her wedges, and she's freezing.

Once they stop, Tor throws both bags inside the back of a jet-black SUV and helps her get into the back. Once the doors close, the driver pulls off.

Jaamini huffs loudly and massages her aching arms. Her head is thumping, and her hands are shaking from the warmth of her gun.

"Cleanup is already on the way. They are much more efficient than they should be. Kind of scary if you ask me," Tor says.

"Tor, right?" she says. He nods as if she should not be asking. "I . . . don't think I was ready."

His brows furrow, and he takes her hand. Her eyes narrow in on one of the rose tattoos covering the back of his hand. The petals fall away and decorate his fingers. His nails are clean and almond shaped.

"Okay?" he says.

Jaamini tears her gaze from his hand and looks up at him. "Sorry?"

He chuckles and relaxes into the back seat. "You have to make sacrifices for your people no matter the consequences."

Jaamini stares out the window, the glint in her hazel eyes snuffed out with her cloudy thoughts. "I don't know," she mumbles, mainly to herself. Tor pats her shoulder and dips his head into her view.

"You shouldn't have to know everything. That's what life is about. Exploration."

Jaamini chuckles to herself. "Are you reading out of some self-help book or something?"

His smile falters, and he gets serious. "Was it obvious?" he deadpans.

She starts to laugh again. Her shoulders slump, and her eyes get heavy.

"I've had enough for today," Jaamini says.

"Lucky for you, there're only two stops left," Tor says.

"*Dio mío.*" Jaamini groans and watches the buildings blend together.

Once the dock comes into view, Jaamini refastens the

straps of her wedges and throws her gloves on top of the bags.

"Everyone else is already here," she says softly, leaning forward to look at them. They laze against the car, waiting.

Sey bites her nails and watches the car as they pull up. The door opens before Jaamini can get her hand on it. Sey pulls her out and into her arms.

"I cannot believe that just happened. Glad you're okay."

Jaamini shrugs, unable to shake the image of blood pooling around her heels.

"He wasn't a threat," Jaamini mumbles as Sey pulls away from her. Sey looks over Jaamini's face and outfit.

"If you say so. Let's go get something to eat."

CHAPTER 15

When they arrive at the restaurant, Jaamini is hauled away from the group into the back. A sour-looking Adelio folds his arms over his chest and glares at her.

"You could have died." His dark eyes are softer than his clipped tone.

"We're in a gang," Jaamini says, rolling her eyes. She stuffs her hands away.

"Your mother's here," Adelio says. Jaamini stills. Her hands fall loose beside her legs. A frown spreads across her face, and she dips her head out to gaze around the restaurant.

Behind her squad are her parents who glare at each other. She can feel the tension from across the room.

"This sucks," Jaamini says.

"I had to sit with them," Adelio complains.

"I have to love them."

He pauses to think about it, and a grin splits across his face. "You win," he says, raising his hands in surrender before holding one out to shake. Jaamini takes his hand and gives a firm shake before darting into the crowded restaurant.

Her eyes catch on people sitting on the half ledge above her head, then on the open back doors that lead to an illuminated porch surrounded on both sides by the beach.

She hadn't realized they were by a beach.

Before Jaamini can plaster on her fake smile, her body seizes up. Her stupid cousin failed to mention this is a family reunion.

Swallowing, Jaamini raises her head and squares her shoulders. She gives a curt nod to Tor, who watches her closely.

She bypasses her squad and steps up to the table. There is only one face she doesn't recognize, and it definitely doesn't belong at the table.

A woman around her cousin's age has her hands splayed in her lap. She wears a tight-lipped grimace and an oversize jacket that looks eerily like Jaamini's uncle's.

As soon as her eyes meet Jaamini's, she gives an awkward smile and looks away. Jaamini plops down next to her father, leaving Adelio to sit next to the very unhappy Spanish woman.

"Marie," Jaamini says.

"Jaamini, glad to see you're still alive," Marie says.

"Are you sure?" Jaamini snaps. Flashes of yellow flowers dance behind her lids. The burning orange of the sun, the wind so hot, so suffocating. Her hands ball into tight fists.

Pinky takes her hands and places them in her lap but doesn't say anything. Marie looks between the two of them before tossing strawberry-scented waves of blond hair behind her head.

Wide lips smile loosely when she looks back to the red-haired woman who's staring at Adelio. Jaamini almost breaks the news that he's gay. *Poor thing.*

The woman blushes when she is addressed, sitting up straighter against the cushion of the bench.

"No, I'm staying for now. I have to return to get back to college soon, though," the redhead says. Marie nods, running manicured nails over unblemished skin.

"Are you dating?" Marie asks. The woman clears her throat and avoids eye contact.

"Yes," she answers softly.

"Cut it out, Marie," Rio cuts in, throwing his dagger onto the table; apparently, cleaning under his nails with the offending object wasn't enough to make his point.

"Uncle Rio," Jaamini says as softly as the heat in her throat will allow. Her hands have stopped shaking; they've gone cold and numb. "Put that away," she says.

Rio's brows shoot up, and he grins before taking his dagger and stashing it.

"Here you are," a woman squeaks out. The waitress's arrival allows a few shoulders to relax, though no one really moves other than to get their plate.

Jaamini waits until all the plates are hashed out to give her order.

"So why are we all here?" Jaamini asks, her eyes sweeping over her parents, her aunt and uncle, and her cousins. *What's the point of this big gathering? Did someone die?* Her eyes frantically sweep the speechless group.

"We're family, Mini. Why else? Besides Thanksgiving," Sullivan adds. It's unusual—she can't feel his foreboding presence masking the tension in the room. A moment of silence passes.

"Cut it out," Marie says, glaring directly at Pinky.

"Shut it," he commands.

"Then move your leg, you—"

"Sorry, that's me." One of Jaamini's cousins sits up. She

can't for her own life remember his name, but he's definitely Rio's nephew. His mismatched blue and green eyes and fiery red hair do nothing to distinguish him from the older man.

He smiles and sits up straighter. It should not be as funny as it is, but when he sits up straight, he towers over both his mother and his uncle. Jaamini starts laughing. It doesn't ebb away until she wipes tears from her cheeks.

"Sorry, it's . . . nothing."

Pinky ruffles her hair and finally takes a bite of the cheeseburger on his plate.

Everyone starts to pick at their food with few words. Jaamini shuffles her feet, tired of the heavy wedges.

"How'd your job go?" Marie inquires, silencing the tiny whispers of small talk. Jaamini looks up from her hands to see all eyes on her . . . *again*.

"Fine," Jaamini says.

"Nothing interesting?" Marie asks, her mouth in a pout. A crease forms between her brows. Jaamini rolls her shoulders. Marie looks disappointed, but what is she supposed to tell her? *Hey, Mom, killed someone today! I think I'm traumatized for life. Thanks for asking.*

"Drop it." Pinky seethes. Jaamini sucks her teeth and looks away. They're insufferable together and just as bad apart.

"Don't tell me how to parent," Marie says.

"Act like an adult then," Pinky bites back.

"I'm more of an adult than you've ever been," Marie says.

"Test that with your gun then."

Nothing happens, and then all at once there are several mouths moving. Chairs scrape across the floor, and guns rise.

Jaamini barely moves out of the way as two shots ring through the restaurant.

"Stop!" Jaamini yells.

The smoke from the two guns rises toward the half floor above them. Pinky lowers his gun first and puts it away. Marie drops her gun, blood pouring out of her arm. Several family members move like a well-oiled machine. They tighten two belts around her arm to stop the blood.

Rio grabs his dagger from the table and tears the sleeve off Marie's sweater.

Jaamini sighs. Her heart thumps so hard the rush of blood is the only thing she hears. She can't comprehend the look on her mother's face.

So blank, so dead.

A streak of red sliding down her father's cheek spurs Jaamini into motion. She dunks a napkin into someone's tea and wipes at it until nothing leaks.

"I've lost my appetite," he mutters. He hugs Jaamini gently. His lips ghost over her forehead before he steps back. Without another word, he throws money on the table and leaves.

The woman whose name she still has not caught cowers under the table. *She doesn't belong here.*

"Are you all right, *chica*?" Jaamini asks, leaning over. The woman's watery eyes say all she needed to hear. *PTSD.*

The woman slowly unwinds her arms from around her ears. Jaamini helps her to her feet.

She takes one glance at her mother before walking the woman out onto the porch and to the sand. It's strange no one left or screamed. It's as if everyone here was prepared to die.

Once they are seated on the porch steps, the woman starts to breathe again.

"What's your name?" Jaamini asks.

"Babia," the redhead answers.

"I'm Jaamini. Who are you here for?"

Babia rocks gently on the steps, digging her slip-ons into the sand. "Rio. He's my uncle on my dad's side," she says.

"Oh. My dad is Pinky, the one with the shades."

Babia smiles slightly, her hands fisting the beige grains. "I . . ." Babia stops talking and shakes her head.

"You don't have to say anything. My parents are always like that," Jaamini says.

"My mother was that toxic too at one point. No offense. I guess we all have a little bit of that in us."

Jaamini nods and plops down fully into the sand. She can faintly see the sparkle of stars in the sky.

Popping off her shoes, she stuffs her feet into the sand and sighs at its soft sinking feeling. Babia joins her.

"At first I was really worried when he popped up. My mother did not want me to come here," Babia mumbles. She curls a finger around her wild hair. "She said he isn't good for me, which is a very strange way of putting it."

"You know this is a *familia*, right? That kind of family."

Babia nods. "Apparently my dad had some very important position in the gang a long time ago, probably before I was born."

Jaamini sits up. Her brows furrow. "What's his name again?"

Babia looks up at the sky. "Robyn. He was Rayne's twin."

"Oh, Auntie Rayne had a twin? I didn't know that," Jaamini says.

"He died before you were born, or you were way too young to have met him," Babia clarifies.

Footsteps alert the two women to someone approaching.

They turn to Tor, who rubs at the back of his neck awkwardly.

"I was just checking on you," he mumbles. Jaamini smiles and stands up. Babia follows.

"I'm going to head back to Uncle. It was nice meeting you, Jaamini."

"Yes, nice to meet you."

Babia nods at Tor and wipes herself off before reentering the restaurant.

"Tony wants you to sleep at his house tonight," Tor says. Jaamini nods, wiping the sand from her pretty dress. She changed in the car after meeting up with her squad.

"You did great tonight," he says.

"Thanks." The two look at nothing, listening to the low chatter of people as they clean up their tables and head out the door. Tony pops up at the doorway, waiting for her.

"Goodbye," Jaamini says.

"Uh . . . yeah." Tor stands there looking at the beach. Once the wedges are refastened on her feet, she waits for him to move.

He chuckles and quickly steps out of the way, almost knocking into an older couple. He mutters apologies before staring out at the sea. Jaamini follows Tony out of the restaurant to the car.

CHAPTER 16

Jaamini wakes up to a phone call. Her eyes burn as they adjust to the brightness of her screen. She picks it up. It reads *Marie* across the top. With a sigh, she answers, pushing the warm cell against half her ear.

"Morning," Jaamini croaks.

"How are you, baby?" Marie asks.

"I didn't get shot," Jaamini deadpans. The line goes silent for a long minute.

"Your father's just not in the mood to talk like a person. It's not really his fault."

Jaamini pulls the phone from the side of her head and makes a face. *She must not have gone through the same sequence of events.*

"Sure," Jaamini says.

"That isn't why I called," Marie says.

With a sigh, Jaamini rolls over and sinks farther into the mattress. It seems to have gotten even more comfortable now that she's awake again.

"What?" Jaamini asks, instantly regretting her slip in tone. Her mother huffs.

"Pinky found out something about that guy from yesterday. You're going to want to be around to hear it."

Jaamini rolls her eyes. *This couldn't wait?*

With a grunt, she sits up and gazes out into the black sky.

"This is how important?" Jaamini asks.

"Deadly."

With a frown, Jaamini runs her hand through her hair and works the knots with her fingers. "I guess I'll get ready."

"Good. Tony says he'll drive you," Marie concludes.

Jaamini pinches the bridge of her nose. "All right, see you ASAP."

"No one says that."

"You're like forty. How would you know?" Jaamini asks.

Her mother gasps while she hangs up the phone.

Don't wake me.

Jaamini buries her body under the fluffy covers and closes her eyes. A rough rasp makes her eyes shoot open.

"Yes?" she asks with a groan. Jaamini turns toward the sliver of light filtering into the room. Tony grimaces when he sees her.

"Did your mother call?" he asks quietly.

"I'm getting up," Jaamini says, closing her eyes.

"It's about Tor."

She can hear the smirk in his voice. Cracking one eye open, she waits a few moments before shrugging and sitting up again.

"I'll be ready in five," she says.

Tony's response is the click of the door, blanketing her in darkness. She isn't very appreciative of interrupted sleep; that much is evident.

Once she's ready, dressed in leggings and a heavy sweater, she makes for the door.

Adelio looks absolutely wrecked, his hair flying in all

different directions. But he's dressed and holding two insulated bottles. She can safely assume they're both his.

They get strapped into Tony's chilled car. He starts up the heater and radio.

Jaamini closes her eyes and sighs into the heated seat. The drive is shorter than she remembers, or maybe she fell asleep. She isn't too sure, but the instant they arrive, everyone is alert.

Several cars are parked outside the house, and the living room lights are on. The three trudge up to the house and step inside. They look around for Pinky but instead just find one another.

Marie steps into the room beside Helena, both with matching blank faces. Sullivan steps in next followed by the biggest, ballsiest person of all: her father.

He stuffs his hands into his ripped jeans and leans against the wall. His leather jacket crinkles under the pressure. It's starting to get too cold for them to be walking around without a coat, but it isn't like Jaamini owns many.

"Someone in this room is a mole. I will give you five seconds to come out and say it so I may peacefully castrate you."

Jaamini frowns at his word choice.

Castrate means the mole is male. Male means . . .

Everyone gazes around the room.

Pinky sighs, lifting off the wall.

"One."

No one moves; they don't even blink.

"Two."

Hands start shifting toward concealed weapons. No one can see the whites of his eyes behind his shades.

"Three."

"Oh god. Just tell us who it is!" Sey shrieks. As tired as

she looks, she's dressed in pantyhose, tall black heels, and a trench coat. Jaamini doesn't want to know why . . .

"Four."

Tor stands with his hands raised. Several heads swerve toward him, but he and Jaamini make eye contact. *The poor guy. And I thought what I did was bad.* Not finishing a mission, going against her parents' wishes, being a brat, and breaking the loyalty of her family.

She's surprised he's still standing here, alive. *It's always the cute ones.* She shakes her head internally and waits for someone to react. Before she makes her own move to shoot, she sees Sullivan's hand up.

"Who cares why he's here? None of that is of relevance anymore. He works for me," Sullivan says. Everyone turns their attention to him.

"Were you a mole before or after you got your job?" Tony asks.

Jaamini looks warily at Tony. His blue eyes are glassy and angry. It's a look only a killer can give.

"Before," Tor answers. Tony seems to relax after that, but only a smidge.

"He's useful. Now, on to other matters. What have you got for us?" Sullivan asks, looking at Sey.

"We ran into a bit of trouble grabbing the briefcase, but we have it. It had exactly what you asked for," Sey says, shrugging. She pulls the case from under her seat on the couch.

"Good," Sullivan chirps.

Jaamini looks to her father. The rage boils off him in waves. He turns and leaves the room. Jaamini looks in everyone's eyes.

Sullivan shuffles through the briefcase's contents. His dark eyes glow, and he scratches his beard.

"Well, boy, I think I've found the perfect way for you to prove yourself," Sullivan says, stepping into Tor's personal space. "Will you take the job?"

"Yes, sir." Tor stands up straighter and squares his shoulders. Sullivan turns to everyone.

"This means it's time." He crosses the room and snatches Jaamini into a side hug. Marie moves forward but is halted by Helena. "It's time for your big day, my darling. The most glorious day of the South Sanz will be all your doing."

Jaamini gulps, resituating herself after he lets go.

"Go on, little birds. Sleep well tonight. The fun has only just begun."

Jaamini shakes her head. She'll do anything for her family, but Sullivan is no doubt a madman.

Her eyes lock with Tor's. He does not avert his gaze. The sadness in them is so strong and so apparent it sucks her breath away.

Marie tugs on Jaamini's sleeve but cannot break their gazes. She is the last to step out of the room, leaving them alone. Jaamini waits until the front door clicks to let go of his gaze.

"Why did you want to speak with me?" she asks into the silent room. His boots pound against the floor.

"I don't want you to think less of me," he says.

"How does my opinion matter?" she asks.

Tor laughs dryly. "I haven't made it obvious that I'm interested in you?"

Jaamini's cheeks heat up. She pulls her hair around her face to cover her inevitable blush.

"I know this probably isn't the best time, especially with a war between your gang and mine, but I don't want to wait until this is over."

Jaamini steps back when he steps forwards. "Listen, I

don't think this is the best time to start . . . talking."

He nods. His hand rustles in his pocket, and he pulls out his phone. The hopeful look in his pearly eyes compels her to enter her number.

"This isn't romantic at all, by the way," she says.

He chuckles. "Better do it before I get killed," he says somberly.

She finds herself chuckling. "Must have been hard on you."

"You have no idea. But . . . this has got to be hard on you as well."

Jaamini shrugs and plops down into the couch. Within seconds, she remembers she forgot her pills. She will be in a crap ton of trouble if her father's notified.

"Sorry if I get you in trouble," Tor says.

"I'm an adult, I don't care . . . much." She adds the last bit under her breath. Tor takes a seat on the couch and puts his head back.

"I was so careful," he mumbles, staring at the white of the ceiling.

"Some things are meant to happen, I guess," she says. Tor sighs deeply.

Jaamini's phone vibrates, and she checks it. She grins at the random string of text messages.

Tor

Waitress

17, and I know.

Jaamini looks at him with a raised brow, and he smirks back at her.

Okay, she texts back before answering Tony's phone call.

"You should come to the back room," Tony says.

"Be right there." Jaamini stands up and stretches. She wishes to be back in bed. *There is no reason to be up before the sun.* "Duty calls."

Tor nods seriously. Seconds later he is grinning from ear to ear. Jaamini huffs out a laugh, disappearing into the house to Sullivan's office.

While it wasn't that long ago she signed into this, it already feels like a distant memory.

Jaamini doesn't knock and steps right into the room.

Sullivan sits with his hands tightly clasped together. A very angry Pinky lazes in his seat. Tony and Adelio lean against the bookcase. She nods at them, and they nod back. Sullivan waves her over with a smile.

"Glad you could make it." He doesn't look very glad, just a bit relieved if she's reading the room right.

"I've already got an idea about what your big mission is. Assassination!" He spreads his arms wide across the length of his desk, then smiles as if that's his very favorite word in the whole world.

"Who?"

His grin falters.

"Right to business, just like your father. His name is Vick. Well, its Victor Hall. But no one cares about that! He'll be dead." Sullivan laughs so hard tears spring to the corners of his eyes. Pinky sits up in his chair.

"When's she going in?" Pinky inquires. Tony and Adelio lean in as well, trying to play it off as getting closer to each other.

"Vick's birthday! There's no better time to test the boy's loyalty," Sullivan says.

CHAPTER 17

"Sullivan," Pinky says in a warning tone.

"She already signed on," Sullivan says.

"It's a shit show. A slug house full of Vipers from top to bottom," Pinky counters.

"There's no better person."

Pinky has something to say, but a slanted look from Sullivan stops him. Jaamini wonders almost aloud what kind of dynamic they really have. The older she gets, the less her father seems like a brother and more like a privileged son. Jaamini plops her hand down on her father's knee.

"Any sacrifice is one I will make for my family."

His eyes lower, and a deep sigh slips past his lips. "You're going to have to work with that rat," he says.

"A day ago he was just another member. Why not give him the respect of a human at least?"

Pinky shakes his head and stands up. "I refuse. I am coming on the mission."

"You can't," Jaamini proclaims, standing up. "My job, my mission. I understand your concern, but I didn't graduate top of my class so that I could let my father take care of all of my responsibility. Just let me do this."

Pinky groans and shakes his head.

"*Hermano*, this can't be the only way. We can make a statement in any form, at any time."

Sullivan leans back on the heels of his shoes. He straightens the cuff of his suit. "They're in the way. If we don't do this now, we'll regret it later. This is the *final* decision. No more talking." He points toward the door, and several people move at once.

Pinky remains.

Jaamini glances back at her father. She sighs, leaving the room. Her hands shake in the wake of their conversation.

Tony wraps his arm over hers.

"Smile, babes. Pinky is smart enough not to get himself killed."

Jaamini nods, her stomach churning slowly.

Maybe that's so, but recently I can't be too sure. She's not sure about anything.

The three of them head to the front. Tor isn't in the room, but he left a note. Adelio sees it first and grabs it from the coffee table.

"Tor says he's going to the store," Adelio says.

Jaamini furrows her brows. *Why would he leave that note? Did he leave it for me?* She scoffs loudly. Of course he didn't leave it for her. It's not like she matters anyway.

With more of a flourish than necessary, she lets go of Tony's arm and steps out into the morning's first light.

She stops on the steps and breathes deeply. The cold air is getting to her. Her head and chest pound. She feels high and dizzy.

Shaking her head, she waits it out. The prickling skin, the aching chest, the watering eyes. She breathes and breathes until it comes back naturally, where she doesn't have to think to do it.

Jaamini steps onto the walkway and up to the fence. Tor is sitting on the hood of his car watching the sky.

Jaamini joins him by the side of the car. Her hazel eyes sweep over his brown skin, admiring how smooth it looks, and the dark tattoos on his neck. One of the tattoos is a date.

Tor turns his head, finally acknowledging her.

"I know how to complete your mission," he says. She nods, keeping her gaze from his. "You're going to be my plus-one."

"Plus-one?" Jaamini asks. Her throat is getting dry, and she's starting to shake, but for completely different reasons than on the porch.

"Yeah." He pulls his heavy jacket from his body and thrusts it toward her. She gives him a nod and pulls it on. He slides off the car and opens the door. Warm air seeps out against her.

She plunges inside and sinks into its warmth. *I need my own jacket. What is wrong with me?*

Tor joins her and turns the heat up.

"My boss, the big boss, is having a birthday party in about two, maybe three days."

Jaamini freezes. That's soon.

"If you get your orders from the boss, I can take you there to the casino where the party is taking place."

Jaamini hangs her head.

It's really happening. I have to take out the boss by myself. She smacks her hands against her face in two pats.

"Are you sure? These are your family, your friends," she says.

"I joined the gang for money. I have that now. I don't need them."

"They're going to die. Tor, this is bigger than a small

amount of cash and a nice car," she says.

"How about you? Are you really okay with this?"

"I knew what I was signing up for."

Tor frowns and rolls down his window. He points toward a group of skyscrapers blocking the rising sun.

"You see that one in the middle?"

Jaamini eyes the tallest building. "Yes," she says, leaning forward to see the building better.

"It's like that. Dead smack in the middle of the city. Whatever you wind up doing might kill more than just the people in there. You have to live with that."

Jaamini gulps and sits back. Flashes of red soaking into the bottom of her heels makes her shudder.

"Thousands of people will die," Tor says.

Closing her eyes, Jaamini breathes deeply. Her ears are hot, her chest hurts, and her stomach left her days ago.

She has to do it. No one else is willing, and Sullivan wants this bad enough to face the wrath of an angry father. This is for the gang, *la familia*.

"Okay," Jaamini mumbles.

A knock on the window startles the two of them. Jaamini rolls her window down, and Tony leans in.

"Sullivan wants to talk to you, Tor. Jaamini, you've got to come back to the house for a second."

Jaamini nods and looks at Tor once more. "Talk to you soon," she says. He grins.

Jaamini gets out and follows Tony to his car.

"You forgot to take your medication," Tony says, popping the passenger door open for her. She gets in and readjusts herself. Her hands stop fumbling with the seat belt, and she stares down at the gray sleeves of the jacket. She fans her hot face.

"Hot now, are you?" Tony asks, smirking at her while he

gets in. He sticks the key into the ignition but doesn't turn it. She looks away, knowing she's most likely blushing.

"Are you wearing his jacket?" Tony inquires softly. Jaamini clears her throat and relaxes her face. She's most likely still blushing, but she ignores that and concentrates on the facts.

"I was cold, so he offered it to me."

"So, yes," Tony says. He offers a knowing look.

Jaamini confirms with a nod. She clasps her hands together in her lap. His jacket is so much bigger than she is. It swallows her shape away. She can't find her arms or hands under all the fabric. Another moment passes.

"Are you going to give it back?" Tony asks. He grins wolfishly.

Jaamini practically jumps out of the car and runs up to the house. The door swings open when she reaches for it. Tor is already on his way out. His frown twists upward, and he raises a brow.

"Back so soon, love?"

She chuckles and strips off the jacket. His smirk fades, and he takes it back.

"Sorry, I forgot I was wearing it," she says.

"You can keep it until you have your own," he says.

"I own jackets."

He shrugs. "You know I didn't mean it like that." He opens the jacket, holding the arms out to her. His soapy scent swamps the area the longer he holds it there. He doesn't look bored while waiting. His face isn't changing at all.

"All right," she mumbles and pulls the jacket back on. "I am giving this back the instant I see you."

"Okay," he says.

"Good."

"Great." He smiles and points behind her. Tony rests his back against the car with his head cocked to the side. She runs a hand absently through her hair. Tor continues waiting for . . . something.

"What?" she asks.

"You're blocking the way out, darling."

Jaamini squeaks and moves swiftly down the stairs, through the fence, and across the street. Tony opens the door for her again but doesn't remark on the jacket.

They arrive at his apartment quickly. Jaamini climbs out of the car and makes her way inside the building. She mulls over the day's events.

She has to kill thousands.

How? Why?

She shakes her head, enters Tony's apartment, and shuts the door behind her.

Jaamini grabs a bottled water and her pills, swallowing one and washing it down with ice water. A loud chime startles her.

Jaamini hastily retrieves her phone.

Good luck, Mini. Return home safely.

It's from her mother. With a frown, she turns her screen off.

Return safely? Does Marie really want that? Or would the woman rather I die in a fight so I no longer burden her? Just like that day . . .

Like a movie projected against the wall, she can see it—the large sunflowers swaying in the wind, the sun dropping below the horizon, and those endless hills with her mother disappearing into the fields. She didn't want her then, and she never has.

CHAPTER 18

Jaamini arrives at the airport minutes after Tor. A small suitcase rolls behind her. It's bright red, and he smiles when he sees it.

"Going somewhere?" he jokes, nudging her shoulder.

"Yes. Las Vegas. You?"

"Same."

"Is it more of a party scene?" Jaamini asks.

"Definitely."

The two enter the boarding bridge and walk up to their seats. *First class.* For an hour-long flight, isn't that overkill? She sinks into her seat, her carry-on put away and her hands nervously picking at her sweater dress.

"You aren't cold?" Tor inquires, turning his phone to airplane mode. Jaamini already turned hers off. Her stomach is not having this. She hates the air.

"Jaamini."

Her eyes snap away from the window, and she looks into his eyes.

"What?"

"Nothing. Never mind. Are you okay?" he asks.

She nods absently. He produces a small bottle of essential oil from his bag and looks around before handing it to her. The lavender overpowers the air before reaching her nose. She breathes the strong scent in until her body and mind relax. Once she hands it back, she grabs her stress ball and stares out the window.

Nerves are still tingling in the back of her head, making her skin itch, and her hands twitch, although she feels better and more grounded.

Jaamini closes her eyes the entire way there, which turns out to be a taxing feat. She is compelled to look, but not until she feels the plane landing.

*****

The two leave the airport from baggage claim and hail a taxi. Jaamini snuggles into her coat and wraps her hands tightly around her phone. Tor stares out the window, bundled in a much larger coat. His hand absently twists a Rolex across his wrist.

"Where are we going?" Jaamini asks as they pass several hotels and casinos.

"We're heading to the Palms Casino Resort."

She nods, more to herself than him. He keeps his eyes on the streets, the people, the skyscrapers, and the houses. They pass through a particularly expensive-looking neighborhood.

Jaamini has never been anywhere in America besides Los Angeles, but she can't enjoy the view—not with the knowledge of what's coming.

By the time they reach the entirely too tall building, Jaamini is sleepy and ready to do her mission and go home.

"We only have to check in, then you can tucker out.

Okay, bear?"

She yawns louder than before and nods her head. *Bear?* Her eyes pop open as Tor wiggles the handle of her suitcase from her grasp and pulls her arm.

"Why—" Before she can ask, they are whisked inside by a lady in a full red dressing gown. Her gray hair is pulled into a low ponytail and barely touches her shoulders.

"You should have called us, Tor. We would have scooped you from the airport," the woman says.

"I understand, ma'am. But it's late, and I didn't want to bother."

She scoffs, stopping them in front of a large desk where a lady sits clicking away.

"You're not a bother . . ." The woman drifts off when she finally spots Jaamini lingering around, being dragged by Tor. Her eyes shift between them, Tor's hand on her forearm.

Jaamini steps from one foot to the other, gazing over the walls. The people mill around with a buzz created for Monday mornings, not a Thursday night.

"This is my girlfriend. My plus-one." The woman's brown eyes lose their sparkle if only for a moment. She stands impossibly straighter and reaches out a hand. Jaamini takes it and gives a firm shake, a business shake.

The older woman smiles and grabs the offered key from the attendant. "Here is the card. Have a pleasant night, you two," she says.

"We will," Tor adds.

She steps into their path. "Just remember that you're on the first floor. All the guests come through here," she says, slanting her gaze toward Jaamini like a hawk. Jaamini flutters her eyes innocently and steps forward.

"Oh, they'll be fine. Nothing they haven't heard before,"

Jaamini says, smiling before taking Tor's hand and pulling him past her.

The woman mumbles something under her breath. Tor chuckles at Jaamini's side and slides the key card into the lock. As soon as they step in, Jaamini throws her bags down and plops onto the bed.

There are kids here.

She tried not to look at them.

Her hands clench into fists. She kicks off her shoes and rolls into the cover.

The instant her head hits the pillow, she is fast asleep. Or so she thought. Seconds later, she is uncomfortable and confused. *Why does it seem like everything I'm doing is wrong?* She doesn't want to *kill* people, but it's her job. The job she could have refused. *But then what would I say to my kids? Generations of tradition? I got rid of it just because?*

The Reyes family is too big, too successful, and too proud to have her be the cause for breaking tradition. She has no choice but to do this for her family. Sullivan will be happy.

She has something to prove. *Or do I?*

Jaamini sighs deeply and flips over, letting her curly blond hair block her view of the painted blue ceiling. It seems everything is blue.

"You okay?" Tor asks from his side of the room. Jaamini shrugs, but her shoulders never really drop. Her face gets hotter by the second, and her hands shake uncontrollably.

Jaamini sniffles, grabbing her second pillow to cover her face. The bed dips on the side.

"Hey, it's okay."

She shakes her head. "I know it seems stupid because I don't even know these people, but I don't want to hurt them," Jaamini says. Tor sighs, his thumb stroking her knuckles.

"You want to do this, though, or else you wouldn't have gotten on that plane."

Jaamini sucks her teeth and rolls away from him. She shuffles across the room to the window.

"Wait, no, not like that. I didn't mean that." Tor stands, crossing the room.

He takes her hand and spins her toward him. His expressive blue eyes peer down at her. Her reddened eyes blink in and out of focus. Tor pulls her closer.

"I didn't mean that. You're *responsible*. You'll do what needs to be done for your family, and that's admirable. I wish I had that kind of dedication and loyalty to people . . . or, you know, *someone* in particular."

Jaamini sighs, sniffling and wiping at her eyes. Tor holds her shoulders for a second before huffing out and stepping back.

"I want to show you something, but I need to know that you trust me," he says.

Jaamini hesitates, then nods. "Of course I trust you . . . kind of . . . but my father doesn't, and that makes me suspicious. After all this, I have a right to be suspicious, right?"

He looks away, staring off into the dark night. "Yes, you should be. But I would never hurt you. I promise."

Jaamini takes his hand, and their eyes lock. "Then show me."

The two of them leave the room out the door on the side of the building. As they walk, Jaamini watches the swaying trees illuminated by the streetlights. Her skin prickles in the cool night air.

Tor stops them in front of a shed a ways away from the back of the casino. *Why is it here?* She can't fathom why a big business like this would have a shed.

The shed door opens with a creak, and they step inside the cramped building. The sweet scent of grass is brushed away by the eroding wood and moss.

"I hid it just in case I needed a backup plan," Tor explains.

Jaamini lets go of his hand while he shuffles under all the boxes and tools. Tor pulls a chest from under a plank of wood. He props the chest up on the sole window sill in the back of the shed and looks at her.

Jaamini stands next to him, holding her breath. Whatever he has in there, he's most likely risking his life showing her.

Tor pops off the lid and stuffs a shiny silver key in his pocket before pulling out a roll of blueprints.

Jaamini's brows knit together, her hazel eyes frantically looking over the blueprints.

"Is this the building?" she asks.

"Yes. Exactly where you need to go is highlighted."

The roll of paper slips from her hands and smacks the ground. Tor looks between her mouth hanging open and the blueprints. She hurriedly picks them up and stuffs them back in the box.

"Are you insane?" she shouts. They both look around, waiting for someone to find them. Jaamini wipes her clammy hands on her jeans. "I am not taking that from you."

Tor locks the chest and stashes it back in its hiding spot.

"It's here for you if you ever want it. I think it might help."

"You're insane. Officially insane. *Muchachos*," she mumbles under her breath.

Tor cracks a smile and pulls her into a hug. "You know I'd do anything for you, right?"

Jaamini places her head on his chest and basks in his hug.

His fresh soapy scent fills her nose and overpowers the smell of the shed.

"You shouldn't." She gulps past the lump in her throat, shoulders sagging.

The two of them depart and make their way back into the building. Jaamini closes and locks the door.

"We should probably sleep now," Tor says, pouring cold tea into a cup.

"Why?" Jaamini asks, already knowing why. They will need energy and clear minds for tomorrow's ultimate deception. Her stomach rolls just thinking about it.

Tor doesn't answer, thrusting a cup at her. Jaamini takes it and rests against the wall. Tor joins her on the rug under the window. They stare at the opposing wall in silence.

"Now what?" Jaamini turns her steady gaze to his face. His beautiful eyes are brightened by the moonlight slipping through the curtains.

"Now we succeed."

Jaamini takes a gulp of her tea and rests against the wall's cool surface.

CHAPTER 19

Jaamini rerolls the blueprints and makes her way back inside. The halls are quiet in the wee hours of the morning. Breakfast is already being prepared in the café down the hall. A few kids already left the building, probably headed to school. It was, in fact, a school night. Jaamini slips back into the room and opens up her suitcase.

They were stupid to have let her in without checking her bag. She throws the few articles of clothing out of the way and grabs her tools. She has some planting to do. Without waking Tor, she steps out of the room in her room service outfit. It was in the closet when she opened it. Must have been Tor's doing. With shaky hands, she whistles a merry tune and pushes her cart through the hall.

Not a person looks her way as she wanders through the building to the elevator.

On her way up, Marie texts her. She frowns when the message comes in and silences her phone. Whatever it is can't be important. Nothing is as important as her focusing. If she gets away with this—*when* she gets away with this— she will address whatever her mother has to say.

The elevator chimes, the doors sliding open. The cart momentarily catches on the rug, making her jerk it out into the hall. A man stops to stare.

"You all right, miss?"

"Yes, sir. Good morning to you," Jaamini says.

"Yes, good morning. Is the café open yet?"

Jaamini wants to shrug but resists the urge. "It seems like they're just about ready. Why don't you head down?"

He nods and enters the elevator. She steps out and offers a big smile and wave. The ashy-haired man smiles and waves back. The doors close on them.

Jaamini's smile drops instantly. *Socializing in the morning? No thank you.* She opens the janitor's closet and changes into the maintenance outfit.

The baggy blue jumpsuit and large brown loafers don't fit, but that doesn't matter. She has more pocket space and mobility.

Jaamini hauls a toolbox up on her cart and empties her *personal* tools into the box. Jaamini looks around the hall once more, then steps out and fixes her cap tighter to her head, covering her face.

She gets into the elevator and swipes the janitor's card for the basement. *Time to work.*

The elevator travels down four floors before stopping. A couple gets on, speaking loudly about some wedding they went to.

"Sir, will you press the first floor please?" the man asks. Jaamini's brows furrow before she reaches out and clicks the button. The elevator is silent for a moment, two intense gazes watching her. The woman mumbles into his ear and smacks his arm.

"Oh, sorry, I hadn't noticed you were a woman."

"It's fine," Jaamini rushes to say. *Why did this have to be a part of my mission?* She sighs internally as they step off.

"You going up?" a voice calls. They rush in and reach out but stop when they notice the *B* clicked. The woman who entered eyes Jaamini.

"Oh, hell. It's always the foreign kids taking the jobs," the woman says. She leaves with her head held high. Her heels click loudly down the hall and straight to the front desk.

Jaamini rapidly jabs the door button. They close before the receptionist can get a glimpse of her. That would've been bad, very bad.

The doors open, and a technician stops working to stare at her. She lowers her head and steps off, walking straight toward him. Jaamini socks him square in the jaw. He hits the ground groaning and rolls to the side.

"Hey, buddy, you run electrical?"

He nods solemnly. She grins at him and offers a hand. The man smacks it away and jumps to his feet. Jaamini reaches into her toolbox and pulls out her gun. It clicks as it cocks, stopping him in his retreat. His hands steadily rise, and he turns toward her. His wide eyes close tightly.

"You're going to do something, and I'm going to be grateful, right?"

He nods and waits patiently as she crosses the distance he put between them.

"Pull up the screening for tomorrow for Victor Hall's party."

The technician—Hector, as it says on his tag—turns slowly and walks them over past the security monitors to another desk. She eyes the white coffee mug and the steaming tea on the desk. Her eyes lock on the man clicking furiously through files on his computer. He turns the monitor over to her.

She can see the file is for Victor Hall's birthday. She almost laughs at the kid in the photos but holds it in. Jaamini throws her toolbox down, getting her hand steady, and shuffles through until she finds the flash drive.

"Put this in, and click the program."

He reaches for the monitor. With a shaky breath, the man places the flash drive in the desktop and opens the only file. The screen goes black, and it flickers before turning back on with a few windows popping open.

Do the Sanz have a hacker? Shaking her head, she waits, looking toward the elevator. That's the only way out.

The man clicks "okay" on the screen and waits for something to happen. Her phone buzzes with the confirmation.

Once Jaamini is sure the computer files were set up, she turns to the man. He is still checking over everything. With a deep inhale, she moves before she can convince herself otherwise. His body jerks violently in her grip, twitching and thrashing until it just stops. Jaamini pulls back and uses his coat to wipe off the blood.

His lips move, and he chokes once more before his eyes roll back. She removes her knife and wraps up his wound. Her small frame packs enough strength to haul him into the corner.

Using his heavy body as a stool, she unscrews the vent bolts and places her toolbox inside. The elevator chimes, and she rushes, kicking off the man under her and pulling herself inside the vent.

She waits patiently until it's silent. But no one comes. With a sigh, Jaamini shuffles through the vents. They twist and turn. Her arms get squished to her sides, her hair so long she crawls on it.

She jumps down the first shoot into an office. From what

she can tell, it's the manager's office.

Jaamini plants a bomb on the underside of the desk. Poor thing won't know what hit them.

Jaamini frowns as she shuffles back into the vents toward the other side of the building.

She does this again in the men's bathroom, kicking up quite a ruckus once she makes it back into the vents.

"It's a rat, I tell you! Nothing else scampers like that!" a man yells. She shakes her head vigorously, trying to remove everything she saw. If she had acid she would splash her face with it.

The third sticky bomb is stuck to the outside of the building's emergency stairway. She looks around for cameras, knowing there aren't any.

Why aren't there cameras over here? This is the place they're needed most.

She shrugs and makes her way back into the building. Now she needs a shower. Once she reaches the room, she catches Tor redressing.

She looks down quickly and fumbles around for her suitcase.

"I took the liberty of setting out an outfit for tomorrow. I didn't know how long you would take," he says.

"Did you hold up your end?" Jaamini asks, rushing past him.

"Of course." He points to the small rectangular box blinking red in the far corner of the room. Jaamini sighs, setting down her toolbox.

"Good." Her eyes run the length of the mattress until she is met with a revealing dress.

"Before you say anything, I have a practical reason for choosing that," he says.

She closes her mouth and folds her arms. Tor sighs and

plops down on his bed.

"If the dress is loose and stretchy it will be easier to move in and take off. No hassle. Plus, it may be revealing, but it's formal."

Jaamini rolls her shoulders. Her head is already pounding. She just wants a shower and to sleep. People will start noticing things are off before the party starts tomorrow.

Jaamini gets into the shower and spends little time relaxing. Her heart races with the knowledge she's not done yet. She's more nervous now than she has been this whole time.

This is it.

CHAPTER 20

The two step out of the room together late in the afternoon the next day. The party is beginning soon, and now that they've gone over the plan, they're ready.

Dressed in their flashy clothes, they enter the main room and walk to their table.

Jaamini holds tightly to Tor's hand. He remains silent.

The plates in front of them stay empty. Steaming buffets sit against the inner wall. Servers stand about, slapping globs of food down on the decorative Styrofoam.

She can't stomach to look at it.

Too anxious to sit still, Jaamini looks around the room until she spots the next part of her mission. Tor follows her line of sight.

She watches a woman with long graying hair wearing a purple jumpsuit chat idly with a man in an olive three-piece suit. They stand by the wall closest to the hallway.

"We still have ten minutes," Tor says, taking a drink offered to him by the woman seated across the table. She looks familiar, but Jaamini is too focused on the couple. They and the rest of the guests are waiting for the birthday man.

"No, we have ten minutes to leave. This is happening now."

Tor's eyes go wide, and he bolts to his feet. The others at the table eye him but don't say anything.

Victor Hall enters the recreational room, and everyone shouts happy birthday. Streams of silver confetti fall to the floor.

Tor takes Jaamini's hand and shuffles them through the crowd to the woman and her husband.

Her blue eyes are familiar, but that's to be expected of Tony's mother.

"Hello again, Tiana," Tor says. The woman turns and throws her arms tightly around Tor.

"Hello, second son." She pinches his cheek and turns to Jaamini. "You must be the girl he won't stop talking about."

Jaamini eyes him, but he has already moved on to greeting the man with the serpent cane. A Viper with a serpent cane. How . . . *odd*.

Jaamini smiles at the woman and graciously accepts her hug.

"Not to be a bother, but I have to go to the ladies' room. Will you walk me?" Jaamini asks. Tiana tilts her head to the side in confusion. Her face lights up, and she nods. She thrusts her drink into her husband's hand. Her husband takes it and steps away to take a phone call. Tor sends Jaamini a firm nod, and she darts after Tiana.

"Right over here, darling," Tiana says and points to the sign. Jaamini smiles, though it isn't as forced as it should have been.

"Thank you. I will be out soon. You can make your way back."

"All right. Be careful," she says before stepping away. Right then, her husband shoots out of the room and almost sprints into her arms.

"It's about the surrogate. They're doing it. They're having a baby!"

Tiana's eyes go wide, and she holds tightly to his arm.

Jaamini steps into the bathroom. As sweet as their faces are, she still has stuff to do.

Jaamini waits until Tony's mom footsteps are out of earshot. She peeks through the door to see the couple on their way to the front.

Jaamini grabs her clothes from the vent and hurries into a stall. Once she is redressed, she washes the sweat from her face and leaves the bathroom. She only has to walk straight.

Jaamini straightens out her jacket and ducks through the halls toward the front. From her brief glance inside the room, she can't see Tor. Everyone is still gathered in celebration. No one is close enough to the front to see or recognize her as she leaves.

Darkness blankets the building, sounding off her hasty escape.

Jaamini checks the side of the building and sees that her shared room with Tor is empty. He moves fast, and she hopes he did what was asked of him. Hopefully he isn't a traitor. A mole is changeable, but a traitor is deadly.

Her guard is still up as she shuffles through the throng of people crossing the street and heading to their destinations. With her black tracksuit in the middle of November, she feels slightly out of place next to leggings, boots, puffers, and scarves. Her hands find their way into her pockets.

In one pocket is the last tool — a small red button enclosed in a glass cover, like in the movies. But at least in the movies they look cool while buildings blow up behind them.

Jaamini feels so nauseous it's starting to give her a

migraine. She looks behind her twice. She monitors the distance between herself and the building. If she doesn't do it soon she'll lose her opportunity. Swallowing down the bile in her throat, she flips the clear case off of the button.

I'm far enough, right? If the building weren't so tall, she wouldn't be able to see it this far away. They have to be running about the building trying to figure out what's happening by now. Jaamini stops walking and closes her eyes.

It's just a button. For all I know, this whole mission was another joke. Hot wind wraps around her from the exhaust of a car. *Not far enough,* she thinks.

Jaamini jogs farther, pulling tightly on her black hood. She narrowly avoids someone speeding. They honk at her and cuss. But she can't hear anything. She lifts her hand to see her raised thumb.

Without looking back, she runs as fast as she can. High knees, arms pumping by her sides. She is afraid of the gravity of her mistake and what it will cost her. *Possibly my life.*

Behind her, the explosives detonate. A loud series of booms echoes through the city streets.

Jaamini keeps running, panting heavily. Her feet lift from the ground, and she screams as her body is tossed by the aftershock of the blast. A black cloud of smoke and rubble flies around her. She smacks the ground.

She stands up groggily, blood dripping from her nose and with scrapes in her palms. With paced steps, she avoids the broken glass around her.

Jaamini's foot collides with dead weight. She looks down at a severed arm and moves quickly away. Her stomach twists, and bile rises in the back of her throat.

Holding back the vomit trying to erupt from her mouth,

she moves quicker. Deep in her chest, she can feel it—the fear, the sadness, the pain. She doesn't stop walking until the buildings give way to a dusty road.

Just in front of her lies a big teddy bear, its fur burnt and crusted in dirt. She picks it up and keeps walking.

Jaamini steps out to the edge of the deserted road and looks down into the blackness of smoke.

It's strange that there aren't any streetlights. A faint glow breaks into the eerie fog of black surrounding her vision, the car softly purring until it's roaring with music.

Tor stops the car in front of her with a grin, his white Volvo sparkling even when surrounded with smoke.

Jaamini hugs the giant teddy bear to her chest and gets into the front seat.

He grins and revs the car before pulling off down the road. Jaamini places the teddy bear in the back and gets more comfortable. She can barely see anything from her side window and can hardly see what's lit up from the car's headlights. Her leaking nose is starting to bother her.

Tor slows the car down in front of the pathway leading up to the hideout. Jaamini squints into the darkness until she can make out its shape.

"We're going to get in so much trouble if they find us," she whispers. Tor grins at her, his jeweled eyes sparkling.

"That's the point. You just completed the biggest mission of your whole career."

"All I did was flip a switch."

Tor pops open his door and slides off his seat belt. Jaamini mimics him.

"You're right, and that switch has changed our lives forever."

The two of them get out of the car. Tor's hand finds hers, and he leads the way with slow steps.

A hushed breeze whispers through the trees.

"I know the path. Just stick close."

Jaamini squeezes his hand and huddles closer to his back. His denim jacket is soft under her curling fingers. They venture farther and farther up the mountainside. The closer they get, the more relaxed she becomes. Her shoulders drop, and her gait gets slower.

"Here we are," Tor says, stopping a ways away from the gate of the small shack. They plop down on top of his jacket. "You can see a lot from here."

"Yeah, it's always so quiet and peaceful." Jaamini frowns. Tor takes her hand and traces the lines in her palm with a white towelette.

Her hand stings, and she snatches it back. Tor reaches out again, and she doesn't stop him. He cleans her cuts and precures a napkin for her nose.

"What's on your mind?" he asks, huffing out a haughty sigh. The edges of her mouth curve downward.

"I don't understand . . . I really thought I was doing the right thing," she says. Tor nods and leans back into the grass, putting his hands under his head.

"Life is fragile. Some people go their whole life with their eyes closed. Others find a way to shield them. But the unlucky ones . . . they see *everything*. They're the worker bees no one acknowledges. That's just how it is."

"Tor?"

His eyes slide over to her, examining her face in the moonlight. "Yeah?"

She leans in, grinning. "I don't get it." The two of them start laughing until they hear rustling in the trees. They huddle together, surveying the area. The chilly November air grasps at their skin.

"I just mean that people like me and you have to do the

heavy lifting. That way anyone who isn't ready doesn't have to open their eyes."

Jaamini sighs. "Still don't get it," she mumbles.

He chuckles, rubbing circles in her back. The two of them peer up into the endless sky. A bright light streaks quicker than her gaze can follow.

"Did you see that?" Jaamini asks, sitting up. Her eyes close on instinct, and she hesitates.

I wish . . . I wish that one day the whole world will know peace.

Acknowledgements

Thank you to all my readers, new and returning, and to my siblings and parents for your constant encouragement. I also want to thank Enchanted Ink Publishing for your editing services. You're always there when I need it, with the best kind of help. This was a hard story to tell, and it took a lot of patience on my part. I am grateful for everyone involved.

About the Author

Jazmin Galloway spent her childhood in New York with her nose in a novel. Fiction and nonfiction alike, she has always been an avid reader. She has never been able to hold herself back from the ever-changing lands of the stories she tells.

Jazmin uses her work as a voice, shouting her stories out loud to the world. Visit her website to stay connected at jazmingalloway.com.

If you fancy, leave a review. It is the best way to help new authors, as well as established authors, get their book seen by readers. Thank you.

www.ingramcontent.com/pod-product-compliance
Lightning Source LLC
Chambersburg PA
CBHW030308130626
46549CB00002B/761

* 9 7 8 1 7 3 5 1 6 5 2 2 6 *